Praise
Captain Cockle and th...

"Youngsters from about ei[...] will enjoy
the action . . . "
Fish Farmer

" . . . a most imaginative and readable tale of an
eccentric marine biologist who investigates some
strange goings-on in Loch Ness."
The Irish Skipper

"The author . . . is a real aqualculturist, so he knows
his stuff . . . "
Books Ireland

" . . . a lively read."
Fish Farmer

" . . . tens up would enjoy the adventure and
the technical bits, and would be much attracted
by the cover."
Books Ireland

"The plot is skillfully interwoven . . . with little
educational passages on water-monitoring,
hatcheries and the nature of water pollution, which
never get in the way of the narrative."
Fish Farmer

Also by John Joyce

Captain Cockle and the Cormorant
Captain Cockle and the Loch Ness Monster

Published by Poolbeg

CAPTAIN COCKLE
and the POND

John Joyce

POOLBEG

To Jenny, William and Jessica

Published 1997
by Poolbeg Press Ltd
123 Baldoyle Industrial Estate,
Dublin 13, Ireland
Reprinted 1997

© John Joyce 1997

The moral right of the author has been asserted.

The Publishers gratefully acknowledge the support of
The Arts Council

A catalogue record for this book is available from the British Library.

ISBN 1 85371 701 0

Cover illustration by Jon Berkeley
Cover design by Poolbeg Group Services Ltd
Set by Poolbeg Group Services Ltd in Palatino 11.5/15
Printed by The Guernsey Press Company Ltd,
Vale, Guernsey, Channel Islands.

A note on the Author

Dr John Joyce was born by the sea in Weymouth, Dorset and studied marine biology at Swansea University and the Fisheries Laboratory, Lowestoft, before moving to Ireland in 1977. From 1978 to 1980 he was Scientific Officer of the Irish Underwater Council and was awarded the Glaxo EC Science Writers' Fellowship for a series of articles on marine life in the magazine *Diving Ireland.* He is a former President of the European Aquaculture Society and worked with the Irish Sea Fisheries Board and the Irish Salmon Growers Association, before joining the Irish Marine Institute in 1995. He lives in Dublin with his wife Jane and their children Jenny, William and Jessica.

1

THE CRASH

"**A**re you sure this is safe, Grandad?" said Jenny, as she peered through the porthole into the darkness. Outside, the rushing wind blasted the raindrops into frantic streaks on the glass, and the rumble of distant thunder shook the cabin. On the horizon, dead ahead of them, angry forks of lightning stabbed down from the clouds, flashing on her grandfather's face and the drops of sweat on his forehead.

"Ah . . . it seemed safe enough when we started," muttered Captain Cockle from the pilot's seat. "But now I'm not so sure. William! Have a look on the radar and see if there's a lake we can land in while it's still dark."

Jenny's brother bent over the radar and peered hard at the screen. The orange glow lit up his face from below, like a Hallowe'en mask. Outside the cabin there was a brilliant flash, and the boom of thunder – much closer this time.

"I don't like *that*," murmured Captain Cockle. "It looks as if we've turned right into the storm!"

"There's a dark spot on the screen, between those two hills over to port, Granddad," said William. "That could be a lake."

"Well, let's just hope so, Horatio," said Dr Cockle from her seat at the back of the cabin. "Remember what you said about the dangers of lightning on the way up here! We are not flying in a normal helicopter!"

"Ah . . . indeed . . ." mumbled Captain Cockle, and his voice trailed away.

Jenny knew what he meant. He meant that if just one fork of that lightning were to touch the hull . . . it might burn out the batteries, or short-circuit the electric motor, or do any one of a million things that might bring them crashing down into the darkness, hundreds of feet below.

"Of course, if we were flying a *normal* helicopter and not a top secret invention, we wouldn't have to go skulking around in the dark like this," continued Dr Cockle, who was never at her best early in the mornings. "In a *normal* helicopter we could park at a normal aerodrome, get up at a reasonable hour, have a proper breakfast, and be on our way in daylight. But you had to go and invent a flying *submarine* that *shrinks*!"

Another flash of lightning – closer this time – lit up the cabin, and the sharp crack of thunder shook them like the near miss of an anti-aircraft gun.

"If the *Cormorant* was simply an *ordinary* helicopter," snapped Captain Cockle, "it wouldn't be able to dive under the sea, or miniaturise to the size of a sausage, or do any of the things I designed it to do except fly. Those men we rescued last summer from underneath that oil rig would be dead, and our friend MacTavish would still be trying to fight the Loch Ness monster away from his fish-farm!"

"I can see all the benefits," said Dr Cockle. "It's just that . . ."

The sudden crash of thunder shook Jenny against her seat belt. The *Cormorant* seemed to drop into a hole in the sky. Jenny felt her stomach falling through the bottom of her seat as her grandfather fought to keep them in the air.

"That was *too* close," he puffed as the *Cormorant* settled back on a straight course. "I'd hate to think what would happen if that lightning had struck the miniaturisation equipment in the hull. William! Are we any closer to that lake? I can't see anything with all this rain!"

"Mark my words!" added Dr Cockle. "It'll all end in tears, just like that exploding can-opener you . . ."

A blaze of searing white light filled the cabin. There was a bone-wrenching jolt – as if a giant hammer had smashed into the hull.

Captain Cockle wrenched at the controls.

Dr Cockle cried out.

Jenny and William screamed together.

In an instant, Jenny felt a terrible sunburn – all over her body!

The lights in the cabin went out.

The control panel indicators and the radar screen winked off, and the big electric motor that powered the rotor blades stopped – dead!

For a moment there was silence.

Then, with a great rushing roar, the *Cormorant* fluttered down into the darkness like a dying sycamore leaf.

2

IT ISN'T NATURAL!

Jenny lay on her seat in the dull red glow of the emergency lighting, trying to remember where she was.

She didn't think any bones were broken.

Her arms and legs moved freely enough, but her neck was sore from the way her head had jerked against her seat belt during the crash. From the pull of the belt against her shoulder, she could tell that the *Cormorant* was lying at an angle.

But where?

She tried to remember.

They had been flying back from Loch Ness, down across the Scottish border and back towards the south. She remembered the lightning, and the crash, and . . .

Outside the portholes it was pitch-black.

She smelt a strange rubbery, burning smell – like the time her grandfather had put the electric kettle on the gas stove by mistake. There was smoke, stinging the back of her throat and making it hard to breathe. In the darkness, she could hear the drip, drip, drip of water coming from somewhere behind her . . . something leaking!

Jenny's skin still felt hot and itchy from the strange sunburn. She was covered in sweat.

Her hand went down to the metal buckle of her seat belt and . . . ouch! It was too hot to touch!

"Granny! Grandad! Are you all right?"

Her grandmother coughed in the smoky air.

"I think I am. But my head aches like blazes and it feels as if my skin's on fire. Whatever happened?"

"We crashed, Granny," said William out of the darkness. "We were hit by lightning and we crashed."

Dr Cockle leant forward and shook the figure slumped over the controls.

"Horatio! Can you hear me?"

"Ah . . . another gin and tonic, if you please, bartender!" mumbled Captain Cockle in a very drunken voice. "And then I must be off home to my wife! She'll have the rolling-pin out to me if I don't . . ."

"Horatio! Wake up!"

"What! Where! Man the pumps! Blow the main ballast tanks! Er . . . who are you?"

"Horatio! It's me! We were flying back from Alistair's fish-farm and we got struck by lightning. There was a crash and you bumped your head."

Captain Cockle ran his fingers through his beard and up to the growing lump on his forehead. His palm was glistening with sweat.

"My goodness, I'm hot! Is everyone else feeling like this, too? Are we on fire?"

"Yes," said Jenny. "And all the metalwork is so hot you can hardly touch it!"

"Oh, dear!" mumbled Captain Cockle and looked about nervously, as if a terrible suspicion had wandered into his head.

"Has anyone looked outside?"

"No," said William. "Not yet."

Captain Cockle peered at the air gauge on the instrument panel, but without electricity it was as dead as a doornail. Then he reached under his seat and pulled out a large rubber torch, playing its powerful beam over the control panel, the computer and the radar screen. He flicked a couple of switches.

Nothing stirred.

"Hmmm. All the electrical power is off. The main fuses must be blown."

William was peering out into the darkness beyond the porthole. Tiny particles swirled outside like dull red snow in the glow of the emergency lights.

"I think we're underwater, Grandad," he said. "We must have come down in that lake I saw on the radar."

"A jolly good thing we landed on something

7

soft, or we'd have been smashed to atoms!" mumbled Captain Cockle. "And a jolly good thing the rotors were still spinning to cushion our fall."

He was passing the beam of the torch around the cabin as he spoke, looking closely at the waterproof rubber seals around the edges of the big portholes for leaks.

"There's water coming in somewhere," said Jenny. "I can hear it dripping."

William listened too. The thick air was making it more and more difficult to breathe.

"It's coming from behind us," he said. "Either the motor room or the battery compartment."

"Well, we can't have *that*!" said Captain Cockle. "Catherine, you take Jenny and check out the motor room and diving chamber. William! You and I will inspect the battery compartment. We'll see if we can replace the main fuses while we're at it."

Handing out torches to his crew, Captain Cockle led them through the control room hatch and back past the big green electric motor, following the silvery rod of the propeller shaft to the far end of the submarine. As they went, the smell of burning rubber got stronger and stronger.

Captain Cockle ducked under the last hatchway into the battery compartment, peered at the main battery store, and shook his head.

Along the rows of special batteries on the starboard wall was an ugly black smear of soot. In its centre the plastic coating on some of the batteries was melted together into a disgustingly gooey mess.

"There's been a short circuit," said Captain Cockle. "We'll look at that in a minute, but right now we've got to find out where that water's coming from."

"Look, Grandad! Over there where the propeller shaft runs out through the hull!"

In the light of Captain Cockle's torch beam a trickle of water was forcing its way past the seal in the hull at the end of the gleaming propeller shaft, snaking across the metal, and plopping on to the floor. As they watched, the drips started to flow into each other as the water started to spurt in . . . faster and faster.

Captain Cockle opened a locker and pulled out a handful of oily rags.

"It's much more serious than I thought," he said, shaking his head. "It looks as if the main gasket has cracked. We can stop some of the water by stuffing these into the gap from inside but, if we don't want to drown, we'll have to seal the leak by putting on diving suits and welding it shut from the outside."

"Couldn't we just put on our diving suits and swim to the surface?" asked Jenny.

"I wouldn't like to risk it until we know how big this lake is and how deep we are," said Captain Cockle. "You could find yourself surfacing miles from anywhere and having to swim for the shore. Until we find out where we are, I think this is a serious enough emergency to release the radio buoy."

"What's that?" asked Dr Cockle, between coughs.

"It's a waterproof radio transmitter on the end of a long wire," explained Captain Cockle. "Once it's released, it'll float up to the surface and start sending an emergency signal. That will give the rescue team our position and they can reach us by following the line back down to us from the surface. Come on, William! The launch lever is in the control room. Catherine! You and Jenny climb up to the conning tower portholes and tell me if it releases properly."

Captain Cockle climbed back through the smoke to the darkened control cabin and played the torch beam about, until it came to rest on a red box on the wall near the pilot's seat. Giving William the torch to hold, he prised open the lid of the box, reached inside, and pulled a bright red lever. There was a hiss and a thud far above them, and the "squeak! squeak! squeak!" of a drum paying out line.

"Not like me to go crying for help," said Captain Cockle sadly. "But, this time, I don't think we'll get out of trouble on our own. Catherine, did you see it float away?"

"A big orange football just flew up towards the surface, if that's what you mean," replied Dr Cockle. "But there's something else. Come and have a look at this!"

Jenny and Dr Cockle had climbed the steel ladder from the motor compartment to the conning tower to watch the buoy and were peering out of the two forward portholes into the darkness. From the surface of the water, way above them, the pinky glow of early morning light was filtering down, revealing dark shapes that loomed out of the mist.

"Dawn's breaking on the surface," said Captain Cockle, looking at his watch. "That means the helicopters and rescue planes will be able to take off soon and come looking for us."

"But look at the size of those weeds, Horatio!" said Dr Cockle, pointing to a dark clump of ghostly branches as thick as palm trees. "They're *huge!*"

"Probably not weed at all," replied Captain Cockle, peering out into the darkness. "You always get a lot of junk at the bottom of lakes. Flooded cottages . . . sunken trees, that sort of thing. It's probably a man-made lake over a valley that once held an old forest or something."

"Well, whatever they are, they're caught up in the rotors," said William.

"Yes, I'm afraid you're right," agreed Captain Cockle, looking at the great five-bladed cross of the *Cormorant*'s helicopter rotors towering up from the deck and spreading out into the murky water. "Let's see if we can get some power back into those circuits so that we can use the diving chamber to get outside, cut away those weeds and repair the propeller gasket before the water gets too deep in the battery compartment. Jenny, you can come with me in case I come across any wildlife. William, you get Rover's control pad and come back to the conning tower where you can look back over the stern. We'll use his light to show us the way!"

Rover was another of Captain Cockle's amazing inventions. It was a small Remotely Operated Vehicle, steered without wires by radio, from a control box like the joypad of a video game. Shaped like a long orange sausage and just over three feet long, Rover had already helped the Cockles rescue the Loch Ness monster, and saved William and his grandmother from a giant crab.

Captain Cockle took the two children back down the ladder to the battery compartment and the diving chamber, where both Rover and the diving suits were stored, leaving Dr Cockle to stare at the unfamiliar shapes looming out of the pink mist cast by the dawn.

"I don't like it," she said to herself. "It's not natural . . ."

3

LARGER THAN LIFE!

In a few minutes Captain Cockle had found where the short circuit had happened and had rerouted the damaged wires, to try and bring the *Cormorant* back to life.

But the result was disappointing.

Something had drained the power from Captain Cockle's remarkable batteries. There was hardly enough left even to blow the ballast tanks and surface.

"We'll have to fold the helicopter rotors by hand once we've cut the weeds free," he said. "There's a handle behind the conning tower we can turn to retract them back into the hull. But it'll take a long time. I wish I knew what caused that power drain."

"It must have been the lightning," suggested William.

"It could have been. But that would have put

more electricity *into* the batteries, not sucked it all out. It's almost as if . . ."

"Grandad, the water's rising!" said Jenny, staring down at the floor.

"Yes, we'll have to do something about *that* at once," agreed Captain Cockle. "Or we'll really be in trouble. Come on, Jenny, let's get suited up."

Jenny peered out of the porthole into the murky water.

"It's awfully dark out there!" she said.

"Rover will take care of that," suggested William. "He'll give you plenty of light and we'll be able to keep an eye on you from inside the submarine at the same time."

"Good idea," agreed Captain Cockle. "Come with us, William. You can unpack Rover while Jenny and I get suited up."

So Captain Cockle, Jenny and William climbed down into the diving chamber, below the motor room, where the underwater equipment was stored. William unpacked Rover while Jenny and Captain Cockle squeezed themselves into diving suits, carefully checking the level of air in the bottles and the rubber seals on the helmets. Then William loaded Rover into the airlock, Jenny and Captain Cockle stepped over the threshold to join the little ROV, and the thick metal door to the inside of the submarine swung shut behind them with a loud clang. There was a hiss of escaping air, and the water started to rise around their feet. In a few moments the airlock was full of water, and the hatch at their feet opened into the dark water outside.

Up in the control room, Dr Cockle was busy trying to clear up the mess from the crash. Charts were strewn all over the cabin floor, technical manuals lay open, Captain Cockle's binoculars had fallen out of their case and Jenny's wildlife books had slid into an untidy pile next to the porthole. One of the books had big, eye-catching illustrations of freshwater fish. Dr Cockle picked it up, examined the title – *Life in Rivers and Lakes* – and turned to the page on waterweeds to see if she could identify the huge raggedy fronds of the giant plants outside.

But the funny green tree trunks that loomed out of the gloomy water looked absolutely nothing like anything she could see in the book. Nothing was that big! It wasn't like a real lake at all!

Captain Cockle, followed by Jenny and Rover, dropped gently out of the diving hatch on to the bottom of lake and looked about. The yellow hull of the *Cormorant* with its dim lights stretched above them in both directions like a big balloon. All around them the water seemed misty and mysterious. The glow of the rising sun began to filter down, picking out strange shapes here and there in a dull red light. But Captain Cockle seemed fascinated by the mud. It stretched out on either side of them, as smooth and flat as a tennis court. He put his hand down into it, and hit something hard just below the surface.

"Very strange!" he said. "It's almost as if the bottom was artificial. It's so flat!"

"I don't think we've got a lot of time for sightseeing, Horatio!" said Dr Cockle from the control room. "The air's getting pretty foul in here, you know!"

"It's almost as if we're standing on a huge platform . . ."

"Horatio! Get on with it!"

Captain Cockle stopped peering into the distance, where the strange flat bottom faded into the mist.

"Ah . . . quite so, my dear! Take Rover up on to the deck, William. We'll look at the rotor blades first."

In the conning tower of the *Cormorant*, William carefully pressed the buttons on Rover's joypad and watched the little submersible as it purred past the divers and up over the hull of the submarine, bringing a bright beam of light with it.

Captain Cockle and Jenny moved out from under the diving hatch, kicked up off the bottom of the lake and pulled their way up past the steering propellers, over the *Cormorant*'s broad back. Above them, in the misty water, they could make out the five-bladed cross of the unfolded helicopter blades, the conning tower, and the silvery wire of the radio buoy stretching towards the surface. Rover bobbed around them like a huge firefly and, from the yellowy glow of the conning tower window, William's dark face peered out at them across the hull.

"Which blades are caught up?" asked Captain Cockle.

"The two on the starboard side," replied William. "There's a couple of those funny creeper things draped across them! Any idea what they are, Jenny?"

"I don't know. They're so big! And I've left my wildlife books inside."

"I've got the books here," offered Dr Cockle from the control room. "But I can't really see the plants well enough to identify them. Can you describe them to me?"

Jenny and Captain Cockle carefully floated out along one of the rotor blades, escorted by Rover. Halfway along the blade, a thick rope of plant stems – easily as thick as Captain Cockle's leg, and bearing large curved leaves – was draped across the rotor.

"How will you cut it free?" asked Dr Cockle.

"With the laser welder, my dear. That'll slice through these things like a hot knife through butter!"

He pulled a small pistol-like instrument from his belt, steadied himself against the rotor blade, and said, "William, bring Rover closer to give me more light, then cover your eyes. The flash from this thing is pretty strong!"

Both William and Jenny did as they were told. Captain Cockle steadied his arm, took careful aim and . . .

Flash!

A pencil-thin beam of brilliant red light shot from the welder and sliced into the thick stem of the weed. There was a cracking sound and part of the trunk fell away.

"Jolly good!" announced Captain Cockle with satisfaction. "Now, let's clear the other blade and get these rotors folded away so we'll look like a proper submarine when the rescuers come."

"How will you explain to them that our submarine is on the bottom of an inland lake miles from the sea?" asked Dr Cockle. "You could hardly say you were researching tadpoles, could you?"

"We'll cross that bridge when we come to it," said Captain Cockle. "The main thing at the moment is to get us out of here so that we can breathe."

Jenny had looked away from the red light of the laser beam when her grandfather had told her, staring out into the gloom. All around her, the strange creepers climbed towards the surface. They were really weird, like an underwater kelp forest. But, at the same time, they were strangely familiar – as if she was looking at something she already knew, from a different angle.

Then, on the other side of the creepers, just beyond the wall of mist in the water . . . something moved! Something huge!

"Grandad!"

"What is it, Jenny?"

"Is there any such thing as a freshwater shark?"

"Not in this country. Why?"

"There's something out there in the lake."

"Can you see what it is?"

"No. But it's very, very big!"

"Big as a fish, or bigger than that?"

"Really big!"

"I don't see how that can be," said Captain Cockle. "We are in a lake and there aren't any things that big in lakes."

"Your *submarine* is in a lake?" said Dr Cockle over the radio. "Remember what you said when Jenny and William told you about the Loch Ness Monster! And look how *that* turned out!"

"Well . . . yes . . . You keep watch, Jenny, while I cut this last creeper away from the rotor blades. Mind your eyes, everyone!" And he bent over the thick rope of weed with the laser torch in his hand.

There was another flash of red light, and the creeper gave way. Suddenly the *Cormorant* rocked as if a huge wave had swept past.

"Now, what was *that*!" exclaimed Dr Cockle.

Captain Cockle peered nervously into the misty water.

"Probably just the rotor blades springing free of

the weed," he said. "Jenny, you'd better get inside now. I'll fold up the blades using the crank handle on the conning tower."

"But what about the leak?"

Captain Cockle was still looking about nervously.

"Ah . . . we'll fix that when we're on the surface . . . get inside . . . quickly, now!" Jenny sensed the concern in her grandfather's voice and stepped off the deck of the *Cormorant*, sinking down over the hull, towards the flat muddy bottom and the safety of the diving chamber hatch.

Back in the control room, Dr Cockle was flicking through Jenny's book on pond life looking for pictures of freshwater weeds. Her eyes went up and down from the pages to the misty world outside the porthole and back. Time and time again, she compared the drawings and pictures with the huge leafy creepers her husband had just cleared from the rotor blades.

But nothing in the book was that big!

Then, just as Captain Cockle had folded the rotor blades and shut them back into the long bulge along the deck, she said cautiously, "You know, Horatio, those weeds look for all the world like something called *Elodea canadensis*."

"What?" asked William over the radio.

"Isn't that 'Canadian pondweed'?" asked Jenny. "The stuff you get in pet shops to put in with your goldfish?"

"But that's impossible!" insisted Dr Cockle, running her finger down the book's written description of the plant. "It says here that this sort of weed only grows a few feet long, at best. The fronds we're looking at are sixty feet long if they're an inch!"

"Could it be a new species?" suggested Jenny from the bed of the lake. "You could call it *Jenifferous enormous*, after me."

Captain Cockle had been strangely quiet all this time, apart from a few of the "er . . . um . . . yes, well" noises he usually made when he was thinking hard.

"Ah . . . Catherine, I think I know why all these weeds and things look so strange to us . . ."

There was a terrified shriek over the radio.

"Help! Granddad! It's got me!"

"Jenny!"

"Oh, my goodness . . ."

On the video screen showing the view from Rover's camera, Dr Cockle was watching a huge scorpion, as big as a large dog, attacking Jenny. The whole lower edge of its jaw had folded out into a crablike claw and was clamped around the boot of her diving suit as she tried to pull herself back to safety inside the diving hatch. The insect's powerful legs were scrabbling on the bottom as it tried to haul Jenny away from the safety of the submarine into the dark mass of weeds.

"Hold on, Jenny. I'm coming!" cried Captain

Cockle, and dived down from the deck of the *Cormorant* into the pool of light from Rover's flood lamp, where Jenny was battling with the nightmare insect.

Jenny's hold on the rim of the diving chamber was loosening.

Her fingers were being wrenched out of their sockets and she could feel the sharp jaws of the terrible insect starting to tear through the fabric of her diving suit. Her breath came in gasps, fogging the glass of her face-plate and making it impossible to see . . .

"Grandad!"

Captain Cockle pulled the laser torch from his belt and peered desperately into the cloud of swirling mud where Jenny and the insect were fighting. In the fog, it was difficult to see where the insect stopped and Jenny began. So he rushed forward, felt the hard, squirming body of the insect against his glove, pointed the beam at its centre and pulled the trigger.

There was a blinding flash of red light, a horrible high-pitched screeching scream, and the giant insect arched backwards, releasing Jenny and throwing Captain Cockle off his feet. Everything was lost in a swirl of mud, blood and bubbles.

"Horatio!"

"Grandad!"

"Don't worry, everyone. Jenny, are you all right?"

"I'm in the diving chamber, Grandad."

Captain Cockle knelt on the bottom of the lake with the laser torch in his hand as the swirl of muddy water cleared around him, frantically trying to see where the insect had got to. His breath rattled in his diving helmet as he turned his head this way and that, trying to cover all sides at once.

The attack could come from any direction!

Then slowly, the weak current carried the cloud of mud away, and out of the murk the hard body of the terrible insect appeared, scuttling back into the safety of the weeds.

Captain Cockle watched it retreat. What on earth was it?

"Horatio! What is going on?" called Dr Cockle from the *Cormorant*.

Captain Cockle looked around once more.

"Where's Rover?"

"Over there by the weeds, Grandad," called William from the conning tower.

"Press 'return' and bring him inside. It's far too dangerous out here."

"But why? You said we're only in a lake!"

"Just do it, William. And quickly!"

William pressed the "return" button on Rover's joypad, activating the little submersible's onboard computer memory to return the way it had come. The faint purr of its electric motor reached Captain Cockle as it turned towards the safety of the *Cormorant*.

"Horatio! Look out!"

A colossal shape, as big as a nuclear submarine, burst out of the gloom. A pair of jaws the size of a garage door yawned open to reveal row upon row of gigantic teeth.

Captain Cockle saw a rushing whirlpool of searchlight eyes and giant fins. He saw the orange flash of Rover and an endless wall of flashing scales.

The water surged around him like a tidal wave.

The *Cormorant* swayed and groaned in the current.

Jenny was thrown back out of the diving hatch into the water.

Captain Cockle was picked off his feet and whirled like a bubble in a bathtub drain, up off the bottom and out over the edge of the strange straight cliff to the bottom of the lake.

The gigantic shape passed, slowed, and began to turn.

"It's swallowed Rover!" cried William.

"And it's coming back . . ." breathed Captain Cockle.

4

THE GIANT FISH

Captain Cockle picked himself off the bottom and stared up in horror at the enormous shape circling above him. It was a titanic fish . . . a hundred a fifty feet long, as he lived and breathed! A gigantic pike . . . the most vicious and determined freshwater killer fish ever!

But how had this happened?

Deep inside he already knew the answer . . . ever since the lightning strike, the power failure and the terrible heat they had all felt inside the *Cormorant*. The power of the lightning bolt had energised the special metal wires inside the outer hull of the submarine and brought about a sudden miniaturisation, shrinking the *Cormorant* and everyone on board!

Captain Cockle tried to steady himself and remember what setting the computer had been left at on his last adventure.

A factor of thirty!

Which left the *Cormorant* only two feet long, and himself . . . a strapping five foot six inches . . . at little over two inches tall!

Good Lord! At that size, the pike could chop him in two with one bite of its enormous jaws! And there was young Jenny, all one and a half inches of her, floating helplessly in the whirling currents left by the passing of that huge fish. As tasty a morsel for a ravenous pike as ever there was!

It was pointing straight at her now . . . a thing as big as the biggest shark that ever lived . . . with jaws wide enough to swallow a car! A thing that had already swallowed a complete robot submersible in one easy gulp.

With trembling hands, Captain Horatio Nelson Cockle tightened his grip on the laser torch, pulled himself up out of the mud and into clear view of the pike, and waved his arms frantically.

"Down here, you brute!" he shouted into his helmet. "I'm a much bigger breakfast than she is!"

But the pike didn't see him.

It was rushing straight towards Jenny, who saw it coming and wriggled like a hooked worm as she tried to swim back to the diving hatch.

Captain Cockle ripped the laser welder from his belt, took aim at the enormous rushing shape, and fired.

A piercing needle of ruby light punched through the water, seared the pike's snout and jerked the huge fish to one side. With the speed of an express train it swerved past Jenny, dived down, and knocked Captain Cockle reeling across the muddy bottom, to land upside down in a cloud of silt, all alone.

For a moment, the swirling mud blocked out any sign of the terrible fish. Captain Cockle struggled to his feet in the fog, feeling naked and open to attack from any direction at any time. He looked left and right, up and down, backwards and forwards . . . he could see nothing!

Then, out of the settling mud clouds, the strange black cliff swam into view above him, towering up into the murk. And, passing like the shadow of death along its edge, was the dark, sinister shape of the pike . . . closing in for the kill!

Captain Cockle watched it swim confidently round and round, waiting for its chance to pounce. He scrabbled in the mud for the cord that tied the laser torch to his belt and felt . . . nothing! It must have broken loose when he took that last tumble after the pike had rushed at Jenny. He searched the cliff for handholds to try and climb back to the safety of the *Cormorant*, but it was as smooth and black as a granite slab!

The pike loomed above him, blocking out the light. Then it turned, and dived . . .

Suddenly, as certain as anything he had ever known, Captain Cockle knew he was going to die. His whole life . . . his time in the Navy . . . his life with Catherine . . . their children . . . their grandchildren . . . his wonderful inventions . . . all flashed before his eyes.

"Sorry, Catherine, old girl . . ." he gasped out loud into the helmet of his diving suit.

All at once, out of the corner of his eye, Captain Cockle caught sight of another object in the water – a spinning, flashing metal object, whizzing towards him at great speed. For a moment he thought it was Rover, but Rover was deep inside the stomach of the pike. Then he thought it might be a torpedo, but there was no propeller noise and, anyway, where would a torpedo come from down here?

Then the pike saw the thing, too! It jerked to one side, opened its terrible jaws and . . . snap! . . . slammed them shut on the flashing object.

All hell broke loose!

The pike twisted and spun and jerked, thrashing up billowing clouds of mud and sending shock waves through the water that buffeted Captain Cockle up off the bottom, up over the lip of the strange black cliff and back towards the *Cormorant*.

As he cartwheeled through the water, Captain Cockle suddenly knew what the spinning metal thing was. It wasn't a torpedo, and it wasn't Rover. It was a fisherman's lure, with a deadly three-pronged hook, that was now firmly stuck in the pike's jaw! And, from the nose of the lure, there was a gleaming nylon line, stretched to its limit by the giant fish as it fought for its life.

Down came the vast fanlike tail into the mud!

Round twisted the enormous muscular body.

But it was no use.

The mighty fish was being dragged slowly but surely past Captain Cockle towards the net of some unseen fisherman on the surface, far, far away.

Captain Cockle grabbed a stem of giant pondweed to hold himself against the current.

"Jenny! Can you hear me?"

"I'm all right, Grandad. What happened?"

"I . . . I don't know. But I think we're safe for the moment!"

"But what about Rover?" called William over the radio.

"Rover? Good Lord! I'd forgotten!"

"We'll have to get him back, Grandad!"

All sorts of thoughts whirled through Captain Cockle's head just then as he fought to hold himself steady against the current.

Thoughts of how they were trapped in a miniaturised state on the bottom of a lake, about how they had just escaped certain death in the jaws of a giant pike, about how was he ever going to get his grandson's favourite ROV out of the stomach of a fish as big as a submarine? Well, there was only one thing for it!

"Jenny. You get back inside the *Cormorant* where it's safe. I'm going to swim to the surface and see if I can spot where that fish goes once it's caught."

Captain Cockle pumped a little air into his diving suit to make it float, and slowly followed the wire of the radio buoy towards the surface. All around, the water grew brighter and brighter as the daylight reached down. He felt his ears pop as the water pressure came off them and, suddenly, he was blinking his eyes in full daylight as his head burst through the surface of the great lake into a strange new realm.

Far away in the distance, although in the "real" world it was probably only a few feet, a giant man as tall as the tallest skyscrapers in New York was hauling on a fishing rod that seemed to soar up and pierce the clouds. From the tip of the rod a smooth glassy line as thick as Captain Cockle's wrist stretched down, jerking and twitching into the waters of a lake that stretched to the horizon all around them.

The giant was dressed in a bright checked shirt and jeans. He had a thin, scholarly face, tense with concentration as he hauled on the great drum of the fishing reel, and his eyes were screwed up tight behind a pair of enormous spectacles as he peered into the waters of the lake where the thick line jerked and shuddered. Beside him a giant boy, dressed in the same shirt and jeans and with the same serious expression on his face, danced on the bank with excitement as a gigantic dog, bigger than the largest dinosaur that ever lived, sent a thunder of barking roars rolling across the water.

All at once, the giant pike broke the surface like a
Polaris missile, bursting towards the sky. Then it
twisted and fell back into the water like a leaping
whale in an explosion of spray. Again and again it
rose and fell, each time shorter than the time before,
until finally the giant was able to haul it towards
the shore, where the boy reached out with a
landing-net as big as the biggest fishing trawler
ever carried, and pulled the struggling, wriggling
fish out on to the headland of the tall, tall cliff that
must have been, in reality, only the bank of a pond!

Then, sounding like a tape played on a slightly
slow tape recorder, came a deep booming voice.

"Would you stop messing about, Tim! Can't you
see we have him landed?"

"Good Lord!" breathed Captain Cockle into his
suit radio.

"What is it, Horatio?" said Dr Cockle from the
Cormorant.

"I've never thought of it before, but it makes
sense! Once we are miniaturised, we move a lot
faster than we do when we are full size. Just in the
same way you can never swat a fly or catch a
mouse with your bare hands, because they move
faster too!"

In the distance the giant angler watched as the
boy bent down over the fish, raised a stick as big as
a telegraph pole and brought it crashing down on
the pike's head. The great fish gave a horrible
shudder, and lay still.

"There, now," boomed the massive voice in slow motion. "At least we'll have something to eat today. Come on, Sam, let's take it back to the house and . . . er . . . Mum will clean it out for us."

The giant boy took up the great fish by the gills, his father picked up his endless fishing rod and his vast landing net and, with the dog prancing round them, they turned their backs on the pond.

Beyond them, miles away in the distance, Captain Cockle could make out a farmhouse on the top of a wide track. The giants strode towards it, moving at the speed of a train, as their footsteps thumped though the water like earth tremors.

"That must be where they're taking Rover," he said to himself. "What ever will we do?"

"I think you'd better come back down to the *Cormorant* for a council of war," said Dr Cockle over the radio. "I think we're way out of our depth on this one!"

5

MEDICAL EMERGENCY

"We're in a right old mess this time!" admitted Captain Cockle, after he had finally wriggled out of his diving suit and slumped, exhausted, in the control room. "We're stuck on the bottom of this huge lake, which I suppose is only a small pond, with hardly enough power to reach the shore and certainly not enough power to expand back to full size. There's still water coming in through the stern tube and, what is worse, the rescue buoy is miniaturised too, so its signal is far too small to reach anyone. That means we're on our own!"

"And there's something else," added Dr Cockle with a worrying note of concern in her voice. "I don't know about you two, but William and I have been feeling very odd since we crashed. I think that sudden miniaturisation did us no good at all."

"If we could get the computer back on line, we could run a diagnostic and find out what the trouble was," suggested Captain Cockle. "William, you come down to the battery room with me and let's see if we can get the power back on. Then we can decide what to do."

Outside the portholes, the water was bright with the light of the morning sun. Jenny could see the tall strands of pondweed reaching up to the mirrored surface of the water. Grazing carp foraged for food in the mud below the cliff with their big rubbery lips, sucking up mud and blowing it out in clouds. An assortment of insects bustled and busied themselves all around. Caddis-fly larvae with complicated tubelike shells made of stones, shells, and bits of wood, dragged themselves along the bottom. Whirlyigig beetles spun and danced in the sunlight like huge silvery helicopters, and every now and then Jenny could see a horrible dragonfly larva, like the one that had attacked her, scuttle past on a search for another victim for its terrible, crablike jaw. It was a fascinating, frightening world, and Jenny knew if there was any more diving to be done she was not going to volunteer!

Dr Cockle was rummaging in her medical bag when Captain Cockle and William appeared at the control room door with the news that they had managed to stuff more rags into the leaking propeller shaft and that the computer was back on line. Captain Cockle slid into the control seat, pulled the keyboard across his lap and the others crowded round so they could watch the screen.

Captain Cockle typed MAIN DIAGNOSTIC and pressed "return".

The menu appeared on the screen.

HULL INTEGRITY

FLIGHT SYSTEMS

MINIATURISER

PROPULSION

BATTERIES

COMPUTER

SYNOPSIS ALL

PICK ONE!

Captain Cockle picked "SYNOPSIS ALL" and on the screen there appeared:

HULL INTEGRITY: 98% – minor leak in propeller tube.

FLIGHT SYSTEMS: 100% – rotors docked.

MINIATURISER: 100% – 30 times reduction mode selected.

PROPULSION: 80% – minor damage to main propeller tube.

BATTERIES: WARNING 5% POWER ONLY. Major damage caused by unbuffered power surge. IMMEDIATE ACTION REQUIRED!

COMPUTER: 100%. All systems operational.

SYNOPSIS ALL: WARNING – VESSEL UNABLE TO PROCEED WITHOUT ADDITIONAL POWER – VITAL WARNING – CREW UPDATE 571 – EMERGENCY!

"Oh, dear," murmured Captain Cockle gravely, rubbing his beard.

"Whatever is 'crew update 571'?" asked Dr Cockle, catching the concern in his voice.

"It's a programme I designed to control the rate of miniaturisation so that we don't overheat," replied Captain Cockle slowly, as if something terrible was just dawning on him. "When you push the atoms of anything closer together during miniaturisation, you create a lot of heat. Too much heat, too quickly, can be dangerous. So I built in a lot of safety factors and back-up systems. I even had back-ups to the back-up systems, so I expect the computer's just playing safe and warning us about some minor little thing. There's probably nothing to worry about."

"Let's see, anyway," insisted Dr Cockle and reached over to press a key on the keyboard.

Up on the screen came a message that made everybody's blood run cold . . .

CREW UPDATE 571

MEDICAL EMERGENCY – OVERHEATING CAUSED BY RAPID MINIATURISATION HAS COMPROMISED ATOMIC STRUCTURE OF VEHICLE AND CREW!

INITIATE REVERSE PROCEDURE WITHIN TWELVE HOURS OR PROCESS WILL BE IRREVERSIBLE!

SAFETY MARGIN ELAPSED: 1 HOUR 5 MINUTES AND COUNTING

TIME REMAINING: 10 HOURS 55 MINUTES

REPEAT – MEDICAL EMERGENCY

"Oh, dear!" breathed Captain Cockle.

"What does it mean?" asked Jenny.

"Obviously the lightning strike overloaded the miniaturiser and made us shrink so fast that our atoms were pressed together too quickly!" said Captain Cockle sadly. "Unless we can get enough electricity back into the batteries and use the miniaturiser to expand to full size within ten hours and fifty-five minutes, we will be stuck like this forever! I'm sorry, everyone, but I've got us into a fine mess this time and I don't know if there's a way out."

"Well, we really are in a pickle!" said Dr Cockle. "But I knew when I married you that life was never going to be dull. There was that time with the laser-powered can-opener that . . ."

"I wish you wouldn't keep going on about that," said Captain Cockle. "All we really need is enough electricity for the motors, and then we can use the rotor blades to fly us to wherever there is enough electricity to power the miniaturiser."

"But where are we going to get electricity from?" asked William.

Dr Cockle was still staring at the computer screen.

"There are probably all sorts of things we could tap into if we could get up off the bottom and on to the shore," she said. "There are overhead power lines, household plugs and sockets, underground cables. Surely, even the power from a couple of torch batteries would give us enough electricity to run the motors and fly like a helicopter for a while, since we are so small."

"But you're forgetting one thing, Catherine," pointed out Captain Cockle. "We are sitting on the bottom of some vast lake in a two-foot long submarine, and each of us is hardly two inches tall. How could we even lift a torch battery, let alone climb a pylon to a power cable?"

"The Chinese have a saying, Horatio," said Dr Cockle, trying to reassure him. "They say that every journey, no matter how long, starts with a single step. We have a series of steps to make. We must get to the shore and repair the *Cormorant*, so it is in a fit state to work again if we can find some electricity to power it. Then we must get hold of some source of electricity capable of powering the motors for the helicopter blades. Then we can fly off in search of a power source large enough to work the miniaturiser. And finally, we can enlarge to full size and we'll all be saved."

"Don't forget Rover!" added William.

"Ah . . ." said Dr Cockle.

"Let's at least see if Rover's still functioning," said Captain Cockle and called up another menu on the computer.

"ROV-STATUS CHECK," it read. Captain Cockle pressed "return".

"ROV OPERATIONAL BUT OUT OF RADIO RANGE. AUTOMATIC POWER SHUTDOWN

ENABLED. TRACKING DEVICE ENABLED. ROV
AWAITING RETRIEVAL.

BEARING 021 DEGREES. RANGE 2.63
KILOMETRES."

"Wow!" gasped William. "That's miles away!"

"It's probably only a hundred yards or so in the
real world. Just as far as that farmhouse," pointed
out Captain Cockle. "But, then again, we're not in
the real world any more."

"I know," said Jenny, staring out at the strange
creatures moving beyond the portholes in the
waters of the pond. "We're in a very different world
now."

"All right, then, Horatio. Let's get cracking!" said
Dr Cockle brightly. "The first step is to get us on
shore."

"Exactly, my dear. Let's see if we have enough
power to blow the ballast tanks and surface. If we
can get there, we'll have air to breathe and less
pressure forcing water in through the leak."

Everyone strapped themselves into their seats
while Captain Cockle brought the main control
panel of the *Cormorant* back to life, switching on
only the systems they needed to refloat the
submarine. They all felt the hull ease itself upright
as the ballast tanks filled with air, and then gently
lift them up from the bottom and the strange black
object they had been sitting on. The thick stems of
pondweed seemed to slide downwards and drop

away as the *Cormorant* rose. Beetles scudded out of their path and the lazy carp scattered as this new yellow fish rose up into the sunlit waters of the surface.

"I'll have to jettison the radio buoy in case the cable gets caught in the propellers," murmured Captain Cockle as they cleared the weed. "Let's leave it here on an anchor, just in case anyone can hear," and he pulled the red lever again. There was a hiss, and a thud as a heavy weight fell from the *Cormorant*, anchoring the radio buoy to the bottom.

"I wonder what that strange black slab was?" said Jenny, looking down. "It seems completely square."

"Now for the motors," murmured Captain Cockle. "There seems to be a bit of a current flow up here near the surface and I don't want us to get swept away from the shore. I'll start with the main propeller." There was a strange whining sound from the stern of the submarine.

"The gasket, Grandad. It's rubbing around the place where we stuffed all those rags to stop the water getting in."

"Thank you, William. I'll have to shut the main propeller down." The loud whine faded and died.

"Try those two steering propeller things on either side!" suggested Dr Cockle, leaning over his shoulder and pointing at the controls.

"I'll drive, if you don't mind!" snorted Captain

Cockle, and switched them on. There was a low purring sound as the steering thrusters bit the water, and daylight flooded in through the two round portholes as the *Cormorant* broke surface, moving slowly towards the shore.

"It's amazing!" gasped Dr Cockle in surprise. "Look at the size of that house!"

Away in the dim distance, far, far away in this new and unfamiliar world, was the farmhouse, rising up from the horizon like the largest aircraft hangar ever made.

"Look there! To the left!" shouted William.

To the left of the farmhouse, marching down across a field into the distance, were the tall skeletons of overhead power cables.

"If only we could reach those!" said William. "They would give us all the power we need!"

"How long could it take us to get there?" asked Jenny.

"I'd say it's at least two miles just to the house," replied Captain Cockle as he peered towards the shoreline. "And, don't forget, we still have to get Rover back and find enough power to fly up to those cables! Now, where can we moor the *Cormorant* where it won't be seen?"

"Over there, Grandad," said William. "By that pile of rushes. It's a cavern!"

Just off the starboard bow, a tall conical mountain of piled rushes rose out of the water and reached up to a level with the tall cliff that was the edge of the pond. To the left of the reed mountain was a neat circular tunnel leading up into the bank.

"It looks for all the world like those submarine pen the Germans built in France to hide their U-boats in during World War Two," said Captain Cockle with interest.

"But who would ever build a submarine pen in a pond?" asked Dr Cockle.

"It's not really a submarine pen, my dear. Probably a pipe, or a drain from the farmhouse. But it will serve us very well as a submarine pen for the time being. William and Jenny, you pop up on deck with a rope and try to find anything strong enough to tie us up to while I guide her inside."

William and Jenny climbed out on to the deck of the *Cormorant*, while Captain Cockle eased them gently inside the pipe. It was a snug fit, with the covers of the steering thrusters just clearing the walls on either side. William lashed the bow of the *Cormorant* to a piece of bent metal on the pipe wall, while Jenny roped the stern to a large stick, as big as a log, at the base of the reed mountain.

There was just enough of the *Cormorant*'s stern poking out of the pipe for someone to hop ashore on to the reed pile without getting wet and then climb up it to the bank.

Captain Cockle switched off the steering thrusters and turned to his wife.

"Right, Catherine, you stay here with Jenny while

I take William off to get a battery or something and look for Rover. We won't be gone long."

"Just a minute, Horatio," snorted Dr Cockle, crossing her arms. "Over the past twelve months we have been crushed by giant crabs, attacked by enormous eels and blown up by bombs. We have even fought and captured a whole family of Loch Ness monsters single-handed. But we have always survived these things together! Now we are in a far more dangerous situation than ever before, and you want to leave Jenny and me to sit here and twiddle our thumbs while you go off and do something useful. Well, if you just think about it, Horatio, it is you and William who should stay here and spend your time repairing all those batteries and things that you both know so much about, while Jenny and I go outside. Jenny is a wildlife expert and I am a doctor. We will go and try to get help and find Rover and see if there are any batteries to be had, while you stay here. You know it makes sense."

Captain Cockle opened his mouth to speak, but then saw it did indeed make perfect sense.

"Very well," he admitted finally. "But, if you're going off on this safari, let's do it properly." And he led her over to a locker at the back of the control cabin. "Take these radio headsets. Make sure they work, first. There, that's right. We'll give one each to Jenny and William, and I'll wear one as well. The batteries are good for at least twelve hours, so leave them switched on all the time, so that we always know what everyone is doing. Take the joypad for Rover with you. That will help you find him if you use the tracking device that's built into it. Now, whatever you do . . ."

"Be careful?" finished Dr Cockle, packing the equipment into rucksacks and sharing them between Jenny and herself. "Really, do you think I'd ever be anything else?" And, together with Jenny, she stepped out on to the deck of the *Cormorant*, to climb the reed pile into the terrifying monster world.

6

A MONSTER RAT

"I wonder what on earth could have made a nest like that?" puffed Dr Cockle as she scrambled up the mountain of log-like reeds next to the pipe where the *Cormorant* lay. "It must be the size of a small mountain, and what is that terrible smell?"

Jenny looked down at her grandmother and out across the endless waters of the pond. "It could be birds of some kind," she suggested. "Moorhens, or possibly geese. That smell is the mess they produce, the guano. It's good for putting on flowers as a fertiliser."

"You could grow a whole flower show of roses in here!" gasped Dr Cockle. "My goodness, look!"

They were perched on the rim of the reed mountain, on the edge of a vast artificial volcano. The rim reached round in a wide, curving arc and in the centre was a dark pit lined with smaller twigs and white feathers.

45

"Down there!" cried Jenny pointing. "Bits of eggshell!"

"Well, I hope they aren't geese," came Captain Cockle's voice over the radio. "Nasty bad-tempered birds they are, and noisy as anything. I don't fancy having a flotilla of geese, each as big as a battleship, bearing down on *me*, I can tell you! Can you see the house yet? We only have just under nine hours left!"

Dr Cockle looked at her watch and then peered into the distance. Standing tall and menacing on the horizon was the farmhouse, miles away.

"Yes, Horatio. We're on our way now," she said, and with Jenny she picked her way round the rim of the huge nest and on to the bank of the pond. All around them tall blades of grass, each as thick as surfboards, reached up into the sky and the earth was gritty and coarse like a pebble beach.

"Over to the left is where the path starts, Granny," said Jenny. "We can push our way through over here!" Then she stepped back suddenly, as the big black rock she had rested her foot on suddenly got up and scuttled off between the grass blades.

"I think it was a beetle," gasped Jenny as she calmed down. "I'm sure it was harmless."

"I'm sure it was, too," agreed Dr Cockle doubtfully. "But if harmless things are as big as that beetle was, I hope we don't come across any harmful things along the way!"

Back on the *Cormorant*, William and his grandfather were hard at work in the battery room, pulling out row after row of the Captain's special batteries and checking them for damage. Before long there was a pile of burnt-out and useless batteries neatly stacked on the deck plates, and another pile that were discharged but which could be used again if more electricity could be found.

"Now, whatever you do, don't knock them over," warned Captain Cockle. "Or the two piles will get mixed up and we'll have to test them all again."

William looked carefully at the two piles of batteries.

They seemed to be wobbling.

"Granddad?" And over went the piles, spilling on to the deck plates with a terrific clatter.

"William! Of all the . . ."

"But, Grandad, it wasn't me."

"Well, if it wasn't you, then . . ." And suddenly Captain Cockle was aware of short sharp waves rocking the *Cormorant*, as if a large ship was passing close by. Then, all at once, with a loud "bang!" the hull of the submarine was hammered by something outside, sending the little batteries rolling everywhere and almost throwing Captain Cockle and William to the deck.

"What on earth was that?"

"Are you all right, Horatio?" cried Dr Cockle over the radio.

"Catherine! Keep on going. Something's attacking us. Something big! Quick, William, let's get to the conning tower and see what on earth it is we're dealing with!"

Between the loud crashes and the lurching of the hull, Captain Cockle led William back into the centre sphere, past the main engine and up the metal staircase to the conning tower.

"Good Lord! Look at this . . ."

William pulled himself up out of the engine-room and stared in amazement at a huge black eye peering at him through the conning tower window. Around the eye was a sleek white head, a black shiny ridge and a bright orange beak the size of a rowing-boat. Attached to the head was a long white neck leading to the body of the largest swan he had ever seen.

"Swans are quite harmless, Horatio," announced Dr Cockle over the radio. "My cousin Caroline had a pair on her lake for years. Wonderful parents, and faithful to each other for life. You should be all right as long as you don't interfere with their nest or threaten their cygnets."

"Well, I'm hardly going to do that!" spluttered Captain Cockle. "The parents are as large as cross-channel ferries and the cygnets are as big as yachts!"

"What are they doing?" asked Jenny.

"They're just paddling around the end of the drain and sloshing water through their beaks," reported William.

"Every now and then they bump against the hull, but we're too far inside the pipe for them to damage us."

"That's what the big pile of reeds was," suggested Jenny. "It was the swan's nest. You stay in the pipe, Grandad, and don't come out, or they'll think you're after their cygnets."

"No fear of that, thank you!" said Captain Cockle. "How are things with you two up there?"

Dr Cockle looked around her.

"We're at the start of the path up to the cottage. I can't see anything dangerous, but we're going to keep over to the side of the path just in case. Come on, Jenny. You stay close to me." And she turned up the wide path that stretched like an unfinished motorway through the tall grass blades ahead of them.

There were just eight hours to go!

As they walked across the gravelly ground, they could see shiny black beetles scuttling into the undergrowth, big bright butterflies flopping slowly into the air, and massive globes of dew hanging on the coarse grass blades. Dr Cockle led them close to the side of the path. She had her eyes skywards most of the time.

"There's one thing I worry about," she confided, "and that's birds. Hawks, magpies, seagulls and the like. They could swoop down at any time and grab us before we had time to run for shelter. If we were out in the open, we'd be absolutely at their mercy.

At least we have some chance if we stay close to the grass."

But Jenny knew all about the dangerous predators that lurked in long grass in the countryside. She knew all about the snakes and lizards, the mice, rats and weasels that might be hiding there in amongst the long blades where she could not see them. While Dr Cockle peered nervously at the sky, Jenny watched the blades of grass moving in the wind, and wondered!

After what seemed like a hundred nervous miles, the great block of the farmhouse loomed close on the horizon. The path broadened out into a vast flat plain, and across the plain an enormous red door split the rear wall in two.

"That fisherman probably took the fish into the kitchen," suggested Dr Cockle. "So that's where we'll start. If my eyes don't deceive me, I spy a cat-flap in the door there. We can climb through that and get inside. Then we can search for Rover."

"Yes, Granny," agreed Jenny, but she was far from happy. Where there are cat-flaps there are usually cats!

Keeping a lookout about and all around them, Jenny and Dr Cockle crossed the plain of the farmhouse backyard towards the kitchen door. To the left of the door, two mountainous black refuse sacks leaned drunkenly against the wall. The bottom of one was ripped, as if it had been gored by a wild animal. Torn food wrappers, old potato peelings and a few crushed tin cans spilled out on to the concrete.

"Hmmm. Very messy!" observed Dr Cockle. "I wonder what did that?" But she didn't have long to wait to find out because, suddenly, from the middle of the tear in the bag, out popped an enormous head. Its long front teeth were yellow and worn with chewing and biting, and its mean black eyes regarded them hungrily.

It was an enormous rat!

Rats were the one animal that Jenny didn't like, even when they were normal size. She hated the busy way their snouts twitched, their dark greasy coats and their scaly worm-like tails. And this rat was as big as a rhinoceros!

It started to climb out of the refuse. In a moment, it would be out on to the concrete and from there it would have them cold for breakfast. Jenny's eyes darted back to the grass, forward to the kitchen door and sideways to . . .

"Granny! Run!"

"Where to?"

"Just follow me!"

Grabbing her grandmother's hand, she pulled her into a headlong dash. She heard the clatter, rustle and crash of the rat falling down the avalanche of rubbish on to the concrete. She heard the heavy patter, patter, patter of its feet on the ground as she pulled her grandmother to safety, through the triangular opening of an empty can of cola!

Dr Cockle had just got her legs inside the can when the rat hit the outside, spinning the tin round and throwing Jenny and her grandmother down on to the smooth, sticky walls inside. There was a deafening clanging, banging, slithering as the can came to a halt. Then the pitter, patter, pitter of the rat circling outside.

For a moment there was silence, and then suddenly the conical hairy snout of the rat rammed itself through the opening.

"Get away!" yelled Dr Cockle and hit the rat a terrific blow with her medical bag. There was a deafening squeal from the rat as it backed off. Jenny could see it crouching just beyond the opening in the light, rubbing its nose and glowering at them. Then suddenly its claws gripped the sides of the tin, two huge teeth locked on the edge of the metal, and the rat began to bite through the soft aluminium!

7

GIANTS

The long brown teeth were ripping at the soft metal now, tearing the opening wider and wider so that more and more of the greasy snout could squeeze into the can. The sickening smell of the rat's rotten breath filled the air.

Jenny coughed and choked. She couldn't take her eyes off the horrible yellow teeth tearing at the metal and the hungry beady eyes staring at her. She clung to her grandmother, who was beating at the rat's snout with her bag and trying to keep her balance as she squeezed tighter and tighter against the bottom of the tin, away from the rat.

Then the rat rocked the can, throwing them both off their feet and down on to the sticky metal. They watched in horror as the rat peeled back a large piece of aluminium with its teeth, poked its head into the hole and pushed! The wriggling snout hit Dr Cockle in the ribs, jamming her up against the wall of the tin like a trapped sardine. In the dim light, Jenny saw the rat's eyes glare redly and its jaws dribble saliva. The stained teeth rose as the mouth opened. Dr Cockle scrabbled for her bag to beat off the rat.

Jenny screamed!

All at once, the rat jerked as it was caught from behind. Its eyes opened wide in surprise. Its jaws clopped shut and it squealed – a horrible sickening squeal, like a million fingernails being scraped down a blackboard all at once – then the rat, still stuck in the torn mouth of the can, swung upwards until the can was upright on its end and it was as if the rat's head was staring down at them from a hole in the ceiling.

It squealed again, and suddenly the whole can was swinging, like a cradle on a Ferris wheel. Something had the rat by the tail and was swinging it to and fro. Its jaws snapped and dribbled, only a few inches from Dr Cockle's face. Its eyes shut tight with pain and its front feet clawed at the aluminium.

"Whatever is it?" yelled Jenny.

"I don't know!" panted Dr Cockle. "But whatever it is, it could put us in another mess altogether!"

"How . . ." began Jenny, and then the rat slid backwards out of the hole in the tin. For an instant, they could see its horrified face squirming and wriggling in the light. And above it, with flapping wings larger than a small aircraft, was the most enormous magpie they had ever seen.

"Hold on, Jenny, we're dropping!"

Dr Cockle flung herself down on the floor of the tin, pulling Jenny down after her as the can fell.

For an endless second, they listened to the wind rushing through the torn metal. Jenny held her breath and, almost as soon as she realised she was doing it, the can gave a bone-crunching "smash" and rattled to a stop on the soft grass of the lawn.

"Are you all right, Granny?"

Dr Cockle pulled herself off the sticky metal and rubbed her thigh.

"I'll live," she said. "Our fall must have been cushioned by the grass. Quick, let's get out of here before the magpies come after us!"

They both peered over the torn lip of the can at the world outside. Less than a hundred yards away, the rat was running desperately towards a thick bramble hedge, chased by a troupe of five magpies that strutted, flapped and pecked at it.

"The poor thing!" breathed Jenny as the rat reached the safety of the bush.

"You wouldn't have said that a moment ago, when it had us trapped in the can!" her grandmother reminded her. "Come on, before one of those birds spots us!"

Sure enough, one of the smaller magpies on the edge of the flock spotted the abandoned cola tin and bounced towards it.

"Run, Jenny! Keep low and run!"

Behind them, they could hear the crashing thud as the magpie hopped to the cola tin. They could hear the clang as its beak explored the metal and then the squawk of triumph as it saw them.

"Run, Jenny! Run!"

They were on the rough concrete, running towards the towering back door of the cottage. At its base was the cat-flap, moulded in plastic and about twelve feet up off the ground. They were thirty feet from the door now, running headlong. Behind them the crash, crash, crash of the magpie hopping after them filled their ears. The cat-flap was too high! They would never be able to climb up to it in time to get inside before the magpie reached them!

Dr Cockle turned to face the monster bird, swinging her medical bag at its beak. There was a flap of wings, a loud squawk, and it knocked her to the ground, sending the bag flying.

"Granny!" cried Jenny.

Suddenly, with a deep booming creak like the gateway of a massive castle opening, the door of the cottage swung ajar. The magpie stopped dead in its tracks behind them, stared up at the swinging door, and launched itself into the air in a flurry of black and white. Across the lawn, the rest of the troupe burst into the sky, flapping across the grass and coming to rest in a nearby tree where they could watch events in safety, like bullies scared away from a fight.

The vast slab of the cottage door swung inwards, leaving a huge opening that towered above them. Dr Cockle took one look at the watching magpies, and one look at the opening door. Then she grabbed her medical bag and yelled to Jenny.

"Come on! Run to the corner of the door and slip inside!"

Out of the gloom behind the vast door appeared an enormous shape. It was a huge brown shoe, scored with scuff marks and as large as a car. With a deep thud it slammed down at the entrance to the doorway, to be joined seconds later by another shoe that shook the ground they stood on.

"A giant!" gasped Jenny.

Above the shoe was a leg as thick as the tallest tree Jenny had ever seen, wrapped in coarse stocking. Above this was a column of thick blue denim, towering as tall as a four-storey building, and above that a gigantic body in a woolly pullover the size of several circus tents stitched together.

From inside the gloom of the vast cottage, a slow booming voice called out in a strange low tone.

"What is it, Mummy?"

The giant at the doorway spoke.

"It's those blessed magpies. They've been pecking at the rubbish again!"

"Could you shut the door, Mum? There's a draught!"

There was a loud scraping and a scuffling as the car-sized shoes began to move. The giant turned back into the cottage and the enormous door began to swing shut.

"Granny! Run!" hissed Jenny, afraid that the giant would hear her and look down. To her right, the colossal slab of the kitchen door was rushing towards her at the speed of an express train. To her left, her grandmother was panting across the concrete.

"Quickly!"

The gigantic slab was swinging nearer, bigger than the heaviest gate that ever barred a castle archway.

"Granny!"

Jenny felt the wind of the moving door just as her grandmother shot across the threshold and dived to her left. With a thundering "boom" the door crashed to a stop against the lintel, and they were inside.

Jenny and Dr Cockle were crouching by the skirting-board of a vast, cavernous kitchen. Over to the left, the brown moulded cliffs of cupboards towered into the air. To the right the shining metal rim of a kitchen sink, with its curving metal taps had the look of a gigantic metal factory. And ahead of them was a solid wooden table as big as an oil rig. Its curving brown legs rose smoothly from the floor to its vast wooden top and, on a slab of wood, like a beached whale, was the dead body of the pike.

"Over here, Granny!" hissed Jenny and pointed to a space between one of the cupboards and the wall. Crouching low, they both scampered across the floor to safety and watched. Around the great square of the kitchen table were four wooden chairs, each as big as office blocks. The giant woman who had just saved them from the magpies sat down on one of them with a booming "thud" that shook the floor beneath their feet. Towering towards the distant ceiling on the other side of the table was the giant fisherman, with his son by his side, and on the other chair a giant child knelt with her elbows on the table and watched as her mother took a great shining knife, turned the body of the giant pike on the wooden block and started to slice at its belly with loud, tearing rips.

"Oh, yuck!" gasped Jenny.

"Ssh!" hissed Dr Cockle. "What'll we do if she finds Rover?"

The booming voice of the giant child rolled at them across the kitchen.

"I hate fish! It's all slimy!"

"Hush, Abbie!" said her mother. "Daddy and Sam caught it for us, specially!"

"Why can't we have nice things to eat? When are we ever going to have pizza again?"

"Because nice things like pizza are for people that can afford them," said her mother. "And, at the moment, we can't afford them. Now hush up and pass me that cloth! There's a good girl." And she ripped the guts from the fish, dumped them into a white enamel bowl next to the board, and picked it up. It lifted into the air like an enormous flying saucer and rose from the table. Then it dropped towards the kitchen floor and was laid down with a booming clatter on the tiles. Jenny and her grandmother could both read the word "Tim" daubed in giant black letters on the side of the bowl.

"Even the poor dog has to eat slops," murmured the giant fisherman to himself as his wife moved back to the table. "It doesn't seem fair."

The giant woman slapped the knife down on the table with a clatter that boomed around the kitchen.

"What isn't fair is that I have to gut fish in our kitchen and we have to live like this, while your so-called partner Dennis Pratt sits up there in his office and laughs at us after what he did to you!"

"Mary, please! Not in front of the children!"

The giant woman rubbed her hand crossly in a huge cloth and threw it down on to the table.

Jenny saw the giant boy and girl look up at their parents, and then at each other. She sensed the tension in the air.

"Well, I think they *should* know why we have to live like this," continued the giant woman. "They should know how hard you worked to build up the toy company and how Dennis Pratt stole your ideas right out from under your nose!"

"Mary, that was never proven. Remember what happened the last time you talked like this!"

"It didn't need to be proven. That model aeroplane you invented – the one that didn't need batteries – he told you it didn't work, and then every other toy company had it in the shops the very next Christmas."

"If Dennis says it wasn't working, it . . ." began the giant.

"I don't know why you defend him," snapped his wife. "And then, of course, there was the doll! The one you named after Abbie. I know he stole that! Right from under your nose, here in this house!"

"Yes, but . . ."

"We couldn't prove it, could we? It wasn't in his pocket and it wasn't in his car; but he stole it, just the same! Really, Stephen! That man has ruined us! He's bled us dry! And to think he is coming here this afternoon! I think we should save this fish and stuff it right down his throat!"

Abigail and Sam looked at each other, got down from the table and left the room, leaving the two giant parents to their argument.

"Mary . . . I . . ."

"Don't talk to me now. I'm too angry. And this fish is going to stick in my gullet when I think of why we have to eat it!"

She lifted the enormous pike into the air above them and dropped it into the sink. There was a ringing boom as it hit the metal and a clatter of water as the great taps were turned on. Silvery spheres of water splashed into the air and shattered wetly on the tiles.

Jenny measured the distance from their hiding place to the bowl where the fish's innards, and Rover, lay.

"If the giants leave us alone we can get Rover back, can't we, Granny?"

But Dr Cockle was watching the water flood into the sink and listening to the roaring rush as it surged down the plug hole.

"I wonder where that drain goes?" she said softly.

Back on the *Cormorant*, Captain Cockle and William had finished taking all the batteries out of their racks and sorting them into those they could recharge and those that were burnt out. On the floor of the battery room the batteries stood in two neat piles, one marked with a black cross in felt pen to show that they were ruined, and the others laid out in a neat row for recharging.

"There!" said Captain Cockle with satisfaction, sitting back on his ankles. "Now all we have to do is find another source of electricity and we can recharge them again."

"What's that noise?" asked William.

From the bow of the *Cormorant* came a low rumbling, rushing roar, like the sound of a faraway express train in a tunnel – getting louder and louder.

"We'd better take a look," suggested Captain Cockle and they both ran back into the motor room, up the metal ladder and into the conning tower. As they ran, the roaring got nearer and nearer.

"I can't see anything!" said Captain Cockle as he peered back into the gloom of the tunnel. "Good Lord! What's that?"

Suddenly, the whole tunnel was filled with a wall of churning, rushing water that swept over the nose of the *Cormorant* and crashed into the conning tower! The submarine was punched backwards by the wave and suddenly jerked to a stop as its mooring lines held.

"Thank goodness for that!" breathed Captain Cockle. "If those lines had broken, we'd have been washed out into the pond in full view of those huge swans. Heaven knows what might have happened!"

The water was still crashing all around the *Cormorant*, swirling over the hull and splashing over the portholes. It was exactly like being caught in a torrential river.

"Ah, well, we can't just sit here all day and watch," said Captain Cockle. "We've got work to do!" And he turned back towards the engine-room.

There was a frightening "snap!" as the forward mooring broke and the *Cormorant* shot backwards, throwing them both against the front of the conning tower.

"Good grief! I spoke too soon," shouted Captain Cockle. "If that stern line parts now, we'll be cast adrift on the pond! William, give me that coil of rope from the locker. I'm going out there to tie on another line before we're swept away!"

"But, Grandad!"

"You stay here. I'll be all right!" And taking the coil of rope from William, Captain Cockle climbed the conning tower ladder, popped open the hatch, and clambered out on to the heaving deck of the *Cormorant* as the rushing water tore at him, pulling at his clothes and threatening to drag him into the dark, dangerous waters of the pond.

"Good Lord!"

It was very heavy going, and almost impossible to get a firm foothold on the deck plates as the water tore at him. The *Cormorant* was stretching the remaining line to breaking point, slipping further and further out of the mouth of the pipe, so that the front of the hull was sticking out into the sunlight with only the stern, anchored by a single line, still inside the drain. Captain Cockle's fingers felt down into the torrent of white water for the ring where the bow line was tied so that he could secure the second rope. For an instant, he let go of his hold on the conning tower to bring the second rope down to the ring, and in that moment a fresh torrent of water hit him from behind, blinding him and sending him spinning across the deck.

His fingers fought frantically for a hold on the smooth yellow hull, but the force of the water was too great. With a bump and a roll, he was swept helplessly over the side and into the pond. As he fell, he heard a crack like a gunshot as the remaining line snapped, and as his head broke the surface again he saw his submarine, the good ship *Cormorant*, sliding slowly out of the pipe into the dangerous waters of the pond, with William waving frantically from the conning tower.

"Don't panic, William. I'll swim back to you!"

"Behind you, Grandad! Behind you!"

From over Captain Cockle's left shoulder came a thundering hiss, like all the tyres in the world being let down at once. There was a sudden hurricane of wind and a whooshing sound like a flight of fighter planes landing; and, when Captain Cockle turned his head, he was staring straight into the angry eyes of a giant swan!

8

BATTLING THE SWANS

A hundred feet above the rushing water, the dark eyes of the huge swan glared down at Captain Cockle. He could see the neck stiffen to strike, and the beak open. He dived down below the surface in his best duck dive to save himself, twisting to the side as he sank. There was a deafening explosion of sound as the swan's head burst past him. The white neck, silvered with bubbles of air, slid past and began to writhe like a titantic snake as it searched for him. Then Captain Cockle was on the surface, panting and gasping for air as the neck started to recoil back out of the water for another strike.

In the conning tower of the *Cormorant*, William stared helplessly as the giant swan struck at his grandfather. He saw him dive and he saw the great bird's head crash into the water. Then he saw his grandfather surface again. William knew that, even though he was a good swimmer, Captain Horatio

Nelson Cockle could not keep that sort of exercise up for ever, and that unless something was done the swan was bound to catch up with him in the end.

"Grandad!" he shouted. But the sound of his voice was lost in the roar of the water from the drain and the hiss of the swan.

William was helpless. Everything in the submarine ran on electricity, and all the electrical batteries lay in useless heaps on the battery room floor. There wasn't a spare volt of power to be had anywhere, or was there? Ducking under the hatch of the conning tower, William looked around to see if there was any kind of portable equipment that might have batteries of its own.

And there was!

Captain Cockle was running out of breath in his deadly game of cat and mouse with the giant swan. His attempts to escape the huge orange beak were getting slower and slower, and once he had felt a rip as the beak had closed on the edge of his trouser leg. He could see the swan's mate come lumbering down off the nest towards the water. Two of them! He would never survive that. And then, over his shoulder, came an even louder hiss. A third swan! They had him surrounded and there was no escape . . .

The first swan heard the loud hiss too. It jerked its head up and let out an angry hiss in return, warning the intruder to keep away. The hissing was joined by his mate and suddenly the two swans reared up in the water, flapping their enormous white wings, sending a blast of air across the pond and throwing clouds of stinging spray into Captain Cockle's face. They had forgotten about him altogether! His feet touched solid ground and he pulled himself, exhausted, out of the water near the edge of the drain. Only then did he look back across the pond to see the new intruder that had threatened the swans' nest but, try as he might, he could see nothing!

Nothing except the yellow hull of the *Cormorant* drifting gently out across the pond. There was a small figure in the conning tower hatch, a small figure with a strange bell-shaped object to his lips, and out of the bell-shape came an angry and terrifying hiss!

William had pulled the battery-powered loud-hailer from its clip below the conning tower hatch and checked the battery level. It was fully charged. He saw the female swan come waddling down out of its nest to join its mate in the search for his grandfather. He saw the male swan's head rise for the final strike. Quickly, he raised the loudhailer to his lips, pulled the trigger and hissed into the microphone as loudly and as angrily as he could. Jenny had said that swans were fiercely territorial and did not like intruders near their nests, but he never thought his angry hiss would drive them so crazy! Both swans froze in an instant, with their black glassy eyes staring at him across the pond. The male stopped looking for his grandfather altogether and turned in the water with a frantic paddling of its feet.

"Hiss!" went William in triumph. "Hiss! Hiss! Hiss!" until he was blue in the face. It was only when he lowered the loudhailer from his fifth long hiss that he saw both swans, each as big as battleships and as tall as skyscrapers, were heading straight towards him!

Jenny and her grandmother waited in their dark little space behind the kitchen cupboard as the two giants argued. Then the giant man left the table, pounded across the kitchen and out of the door into the yard. There was a clatter as his wife slammed the kitchen knife down, the scrape of a chair at the other end of the room, followed by the slam of the door to the rest of the farmhouse, and then silence.

"Hmm. It seems as if we're not the only ones with problems," said Dr Cockle and, very carefully, with her eyes fixed on the partly-open kitchen door, she led Jenny along the base of the cupboard towards the great white enamel dish and then froze. Just beyond the table at the other end of the kitchen was a house – a perfectly-sized house with properly-sized windows and doors and . . .

"It's a doll's-house, Granny!" whispered Jenny.

"It's beautiful!" said Dr Cockle, staring at it wistfully.

"Come on, we've only got a few hours left," Jenny reminded her, and led her across to the big enamel dish, where they pulled themselves up on to the rim.

What they found inside was not pleasant. A pile of rubbery, slimy fish innards as tall as a garden shed greeted them. It was a grey, green, purple, bloody mound of smelly ooze! Jenny turned away and looked at the kitchen door in disgust.

"I'm afraid there's only one thing for it. Give me Rover's control panel, Jenny!" And Dr Cockle walked around the rim of the dish while she watched the little orange locator light on the joypad glow and fade and glow again. As she went she called out, "Ah yes, that's the heart, that big red thing there, that's the pancreas and, yes, that must be the stomach!"

"Granny please! I'm a vegetarian!"

"That's the stomach, and so that's where Rover must be. So please hand over my medical bag and let's see if we can cut him out."

Holding her nose and feeling extremely queasy, Jenny handed the bag to her grandmother. Dr Cockle gingerly took out a sharp scalpel and began slicing carefully at the huge muscular sac of the fish's stomach. On and on she cut, until her elbow, then her whole arm, was buried in the bloody grey muscle.

"Yuck!" she snorted as she cut. "I don't think I'll be able to eat fish and chips again as long as I live."

"Dink!"

There was a metallic ping as Dr Cockle's scalpel blade scraped something hard. Reaching in right up to her shoulders with both arms, Dr Cockle screwed up her nose against the smell, and pulled.

There was a ripping, wet, sucking sound, and out popped the small orange torpedo shape of Rover, together with a dozen gallons of foul-smelling greenish fluid, that slopped and splashed all over their shoes.

"Oh, no!" moaned Jenny. "I'll never be able to get rid of the smell!"

"At least we have Rover back safe and sound," offered Dr Cockle, rubbing the green slime off the little submersible's clear plastic nose-cone with a bandage from her medical bag.

"Here, let's clean him up and then we can store him somewhere out of the way before we go and look for those batteries. Oh, my goodness! Whatever is that?"

From beyond the door to the garden came a soft, padding thud, thud, thud. The clear door of the plastic cat flap suddenly went dark and burst inwards. There was a rush of tortoiseshell fur, a heavy thump as four enormous paws hit the floor, and Dr Cockle and Jenny were staring into the dark slit eyes of a cat larger than the largest lion that ever stalked the earth.

9

CATS AND DOGS

"Run, Jenny!" cried Dr Cockle as the cat began to move towards them. She grabbed Rover, her granddaughter and her medical bag and dived around the large enamel dish towards a narrow slit between the china cupboard and the sink. The padded thud of paws pursued them across the tiled floor and into the dark space, which in reality could not have been more than an inch and a half wide. Dr Cockle just had enough time to drag Jenny in after her when the cat's paw, as big as an elephant's foot, and armed with five razor-sharp claws, shot into the gap behind her, ripping her jacket and throwing her forward on top of Jenny into the middle of a pile of bits of greasy bread, shrivelled peas and a fat-soaked chip.

"Get back!"

The cat's paw stretched down the narrow space again, but fell short. They were too far down the narrow corridor for the cat to reach. Again it tried, and again the sharp, curving claws flexed, but each time the cat's reach fell short. After another few long stretches it stopped and squatted at the entrance to the gap, hunched and ready to pounce, waiting for them.

Out on the pond, William watched as the two huge swans surged out across the pond towards him like galleons in full sail. For a moment he was fascinated by the sheer beauty of the two magnificent birds, and then he heard his grandfather calling to him over the radio headset.

"William! William! Get below and seal the hatch! You'll be safer inside the *Cormorant*. Quickly now!"

Snapping out of his daze, William ducked below, slammed the yellow hatch shut over his head and raced down to strap himself into the control room seat. As he raced across the control room, he felt the hull lift as the waves from the swans reached it. He pulled himself into the chair and clicked the safety belt home just in time, as a tremendous crash hit the submarine as the first swan struck. Anything that hadn't been knocked loose in the crash when they had first landed in the pond was wrenched out of its clips and thrown across the cabin. He heard heavy objects rattling about in the diving chamber and watched his grandfather's charts flutter down from their rack and roll about the cabin. Through the portholes he could see the vast white bellies of the swans as they circled, their wide webbed feet churning the water and the flash of their huge heads as they darted at the submarine. The hull bumped and rocked. The portholes were blanked out by bubbles and the cabin was dark.

"Grandad! Granny! Can anyone hear me?"

Dr Cockle stared into the narrow slit eyes of the cat. And the cat stared back at Dr Cockle. Both of them knew that Dr Cockle wasn't coming out of the gap, and that the cat wasn't going to get in.

"I never really did like cats," admitted Dr Cockle. "Nasty, shifty, sly creatures. Give me a good honest dog any day!"

All of a sudden, the cat broke the stare with Dr Cockle as its head snapped sideways towards the kitchen door. There was a heavy pounding of feet, a loud scatter on the tiles of the kitchen floor, and a hiss from the cat as it twisted, leapt and bolted out of view towards the cat-flap.

"Well, thank goodness for that!" said Dr Cockle triumphantly and took a step towards the open kitchen. Suddenly she was hit in the face by a wave of hot, wet air as the head of a huge brown-and-white terrier filled the entrance of the gap and an explosive bark thundered down the narrow corridor, blasting them back to the rear wall.

"What was that you were saying about dogs, Granny?" shouted Jenny above the din, as the monster terrier barked and scraped at the opening with its tough, strong paws.

"Perhaps goldfish, then?" said Dr Cockle.

"Granny! Granny!" called William's voice over their radio headsets, muffled and crackly because of the distance and the stonework of the cottage.

"I can hardly hear you, William. What is it? Where's your grandfather?"

"He fell overboard, but he's all right! He swam ashore after we were attacked by swans, when we were washed out of the drain. Now the swans are after me! I'm drifting out on to the pond!"

"Hold tight, William. Horatio? Come in, Horatio! Can you hear me?"

The dog barked again, bearing its huge conical teeth in a menacing growl. It took in a breath for another tremendous bark, and as it did so Dr Cockle remembered the name she had seen painted on the side of the food bowl. She took a deep breath and shouted, "Tim! Sit!"

The dog stopped short in mid-bark, held its breath, and sat.

"Amazing!" gasped Jenny in admiration.

The dog was looking quizzically down the narrow slit, wagging its tail.

"Good boy!" shouted Dr Cockle. "Now, can't you see I'm on the phone! Horatio! We have Rover, what is the situation with you?"

"Not good, my dear! The *Cormorant*'s been

knocked off its moorings by water from the drain and washed out on to the pond. William is still aboard. I'm all right, but I don't know where William is drifting to. There's no power and he can't start the engine to bring her back to the shore."

"Well, we're safe enough here for the time being," reported Dr Cockle. "We have Rover and we're stuck behind the gas cooker in the kitchen of the cottage. So we'll stay here a while and then . . . oh, my goodness!"

"What is it, Catherine?"

Dr Cockle and Jenny had turned away from the dog, Tim, and the open kitchen to listen to their radios. As Dr Cockle turned back she found the dog gone, and in its place was a huge pair of car-sized shoes, the twin tree-trunks of legs and the giant man who was peering intently into the darkness of the slit where they were hiding.

"Now then, Tim," his voice boomed. "What have we here? There's something behind the cooker, Mary!"

"Well, Stephen, I already took three out of the traps this week! If it's mice again, you can be a man for once and deal with them yourself. We can't afford to have any more food spoilt."

"All right! I'll show you! Just give me the broom, will you?"

Dr Cockle looked to either side of her. The space where they were hiding was a dead-end. To the left was the solid wall of the cupboard, and to the right the metal side of the cooker. If the giant prodded the broom handle down into the gap, they would be pounded to a pulp!

"Catherine!" called Captain Cockle over the radio.

"We're in a bit of a pickle at the moment," replied Dr Cockle.

The round end of the broom handle appeared at the end of the space, as big as the trunk of a tree. Above it was the face of the giant, peering into the darkness through the thick lenses of his spectacles. Suddenly the huge piece of wood shot forward. Dr Cockle ducked, pulling Jenny down with her, and the pole slammed into the wall above them, sending a shower of dust down on to their heads.

"Keep down!"

They both tried to bury themselves as low as they could in the greasy mess of dirt at the edge of the cooker. Dr Cockle hit her leg off something hard. It was a shining metal bar with a strange head and long metal prongs – a fork!

"Jenny! Help me lift this before the pole comes back."

The giant had pulled the pole back and was lowering it into the space for another thrust. Jenny and Dr Cockle heaved at the heavy metal fork, trying to lift it. There was a sticky squelch and the head lifted, just as the pole came rushing down the blind alley.

"Clang!"

The pole hit the metal spikes, jerking the fork out of their hands, but stopping short of the wall. Then it drew back, and plunged in again.

"Thud!"

The metal spikes of the fork stuck into the wood of the pole. With a jerk and a wrench, the fork was dragged back down the narrow gap and into the hands of the giant.

"Hey, Mary, I got that fork you lost last week!"

"That's great, Stephen. Now, did you get that mouse yet?"

"No. But I'll have him this time, for sure."

Dr Cockle and Jenny saw the great face appear at the gap. They saw the eyes squint into the darkness and the round end of the terrible broom handle, slightly splintered from the prongs of the fork, centre itself on the gap, aim, and point straight at them.

There was nowhere to run, and nothing to protect themselves with. They were trapped!

A loud ringing sound seemed to fill the kitchen. It came in two long bursts like speeded-up church bells, then a ringing silence, and two bursts again, then silence . . . the telephone! The pole fell to the ground with a clattering crash. The giant's head vanished from the gap and they heard the booming footsteps cross the kitchen floor. There was a loud click, and the ringing ceased.

"Hello!" said the giant.

Then Jenny and her grandmother both heard a booming voice in their radio headsets that said, "Hello, Stephen. Dennis Pratt here."

"Oh . . . hello, Dennis. Where are you?"

"I was just wondering if you could come and pick me up from the railway station. There isn't a taxi in sight."

"Catherine! What's going on?" said Captain Cockle over the radio.

"Hush, Horatio. They might hear you!"

"Is there someone else on the phone?" asked Dennis Pratt. "I keep hearing these squeaky little voices!"

"Hush, everyone! Radio silence!" insisted Dr Cockle.

"Ah! It's gone now," said Dennis Pratt. "It must be my mobile phone playing up. Now, Stephen, I have the papers with me. If you can come down to the station and pick me up, or better yet just meet me here, we can get the papers signed and the whole thing will be over and done with."

"I'd really like to talk to Mary and the kids before I sell the house," said the giant sadly. "It's their home too, you know."

"It has to be done, old friend," said Pratt. "The toy company has run out of money and this is the only way we can save it. Sell the house and use the money to keep it going. You can always buy another when business gets better!"

There was the thud of the kitchen door opening and closing.

"Who's that on the phone!" asked Mary.

Dr Cockle risked looking round the corner of the cupboard. The dog and the cat were nowhere in sight. She could see the giant Stephen had his hand over the mouthpiece of the telephone.

"It's Dennis Pratt," he said. "He wants me to pick him up from the station."

"You never told me why he was coming here in the first place."

"I'll . . . I'll tell you about that in a minute." He lifted his hand from the telephone. "I'll pick you up in half an hour, Dennis. We can discuss all this with Mary and the kids then. Goodbye!" And he put the phone down hard on the cradle.

"You know he's not welcome with me," said Mary.

"He has to come, Mary. We have business to discuss."

"What sort of business?" she asked again.

Dr Cockle looked carefully around the kitchen again as the two giants began to argue once more. There was still no sign of the dog, the cat, or the children. She turned to Jenny.

"Come on! Let's find a better place to hide!" And, taking Rover, they scurried along the front of the cooker, close to the wall, under the huge frame of the kitchen table and along the skirting-board.

Above them, the voice of the two giants got louder and louder. There was a crash as a plate was thrown to the floor and the thunderous slam of a door, and then silence. Dr Cockle and Jenny crouched by the skirting-board. In front of them was the doll's-house, with its little doors and windows where no cat, nor dog, nor broom handle could reach.

"Quick! In here! Before anyone comes back. There might be batteries for toys inside."

Dr Cockle pushed on the large, pink door of the doll's-house and it swung inwards. They were standing in a perfectly proper-sized hallway, with thick, chunky furniture and large, simple pictures on the wall.

"Catherine, what's going on?"

"I don't know, Horatio," said Dr Cockle, leading Jenny up the crude wooden stairs to the bedroom. "But I could quite distinctly hear that whole telephone conversation on my radio."

"So could I. It must be that this Mr Pratt is using a mobile telephone quite close by. The headsets we're wearing are the most state-of-the-art the Navy could afford, so they're sensitive enough to pick up his mobile telephone waves."

"Horatio. If we can hear them, can they hear . . ." but she was cut short by a cry in the radio headset.

"William?"

The swans had grown tired of battering the *Cormorant*, now that William had stopped hissing at them. Somehow, they seemed to know that the yellow invader was not alive any more. With an imperious jerk of their heads they turned and sailed back towards the shore, leaving William to unbuckle himself from the control seat and make his way back to the conning tower hatch. After making sure the swans were well and truly out of the way by looking through the rear window, William opened the hatch and peered out.

He was alone and drifting helplessly in the vast expanse of the pond. Away in the far distance he could see the black mouth of the drain, the mound of the swans' nest and the huge slab of the farmhouse, way away on the horizon. On the other side of the pond he could make out a long, low building, much older than the farmhouse, and beside it something turning . . . a mill-wheel!

Then the awful truth hit him.

The current that was carrying him slowly forwards was not coming from the wind, or from the tides or from a river. It was the pond draining beneath the heavy creaking blades of the water wheel on the old mill. And he was being carried along with it!

"Granny! Grandad! I'm drifting towards a water wheel!"

"Good Lord! And there's no electricity on the ship to move you out of the flow!"

"Could you swim for the shore, William?"

"He could do that, Catherine, but he could be eaten by a fish, or sucked down the millrace, and if we lose the *Cormorant* we have no way of getting everyone back to full size!"

"And we have no way of getting to the *Cormorant* as it is?"

"None. Good grief, Catherine! What *are* we going to do?"

10

MAELSTROM AT THE MILL-WHEEL

"The radios!" cried Dr Cockle. "If we could hear them, then perhaps, just perhaps . . ."

"Turn up the power and switch to channel six," suggested Captain Cockle. "That's the one that's closest to mobile phone frequency."

Dr Cockle did as she was told.

"Hello . . . Operator? Operator? Can you hear me?"

Nothing.

"Turn up the power again!"

"It's no use, Horatio."

"Try another channel."

Dr Cockle turned to channel eight.

"Jenny, pull the curtain, in case anyone comes back and looks inside. Hello! Hello!"

Nothing . . .

Then, suddenly . . .

"Hello! Mobile operator here. How can I help you?"

"Ah . . . I need to speak to Mr Stephen . . . Oh! What is the man's name?"

"Speak slowly, please, caller. I can hardly make you out."

Speaking with exaggerated slowness, Dr Cockle said, "Heelloo, I waanntt too speeaakk to aaaa mannn caalled Steeephhennn, whooo livvess aaattt . . ."

"I'll put you through to Directory Enquiries," said the operator.

"Granny!" hissed Jenny. "Granny!"

"Not now, Jenny! I can hardly . . . oh, dear!"

There was a sudden thud outside the doll's house and Dr Cockle found herself staring at a huge finger pushing its way though the curtain into the bedroom.

William could see the old mill sliding closer and closer. He could make out the tall store building with its broken windows and its caved-in roof. In places, plants had sprouted amongst the stones and pink and purple flowers showed in the grey walls. He could see the sweeping circle of the wheel, wobbling slightly as it turned, and now he could make out the individual blades, and the splash and spray of the water as it rushed beneath. Finally, in front of the wheel, he could see the smooth lip at the start of the millrace that sucked water from the pond down into a boiling, swirling maelstrom beneath the relentless pounding of the wooden paddles.

The *Cormorant* would never survive that!

It was built to withstand the pressure of the bottom of the sea, but it would never stand up to a blow from a wooden paddle blade as long as an aircraft carrier. It would be crushed like an eggshell, and him along with it.

"Grandad! What shall I do?"

"You just hang on there, William," shouted Captain Cockle as he peered across from the far bank of the millpond. "Your grandmother has been on the phone for help."

"On the phone?"

"Just go below and strap yourself in, and stay away from the portholes."

But William could not bring himself to go below. He could not stop watching the water ahead of him as it slid smoothly to the edge of the millrace in a glassy stream, shot across, and exploded in a pounding surge of spray. The current was becoming stronger now. He could feel the *Cormorant* gaining speed towards the millrace. He measured the distance to the shore, wondering if he could swim to safety. But it was too late. As a swimmer in the water, he would be pulled by the same irresistible force of the current that was dragging the *Cormorant* forward. And, as a swimmer, he wouldn't even have the protection of the hull from the crushing blades.

The *Cormorant* was drifting faster and faster now. In less than a minute it would be over and down into the crashing water. William looked at the glassy lip of the race for a moment longer, hearing the thunder of the water and the crash, crash, crash of the mill-wheel. He turned to climb down the ladder of the conning tower. But, as he turned, a sudden thundering creak sounded through the hull, and the *Cormorant* was lifted bodily out of the water into the air!

"Wow!" thundered a voice that rocked the hull. "Look what Dad made!"

Inside the *Cormorant*, William had managed to shut the conning tower hatch, clamber down into the control room and strap himself into one of the fold-down seats at the back, well away from the two huge portholes. The *Cormorant* seemed to be flying sickeningly through the air, turning and weaving up and down. Through the portholes, William could see the clouds, the water of the pond far below, the grassy bank, the old mill house, and suddenly – filling the porthole – a single brown eye that stared into the control cabin.

"Look at the detail. Dad's got another winner! We'll be rich again!"

The eye pulled back, revealing another eye, a mop of sandy hair, a nose, a mouth, and the face of a giant boy, smiling as if the bottom of his face was about to fall off.

"You've been picked out of the water by the boy I saw fishing on the bank this morning," shouted Captain Cockle into his radio. "Keep very still,

William. He mustn't see you moving. He thinks the *Cormorant* is a toy!"

William sat rigid in the control room chair, with a fixed expression on his face, trying to pretend he was a plastic pilot in a plastic model. It was not hard – he was scared rigid to start with!

"Grandad! Where are you?"

"I'm on the shore, up behind the swan's nest. Just keep still!"

"Don't worry! I'm not moving!"

"Good boy. Oh, dear, he's moving off!"

"Where to?"

"I think he'll take you back up to the farmhouse. I'll try and follow you both on foot. Just keep still and we'll get out of this mess somehow!"

Captain Cockle finished wringing the water out of his clothes, emptied the mud out of his second shoe, and watched the giant boy stride around the far side of the pond. By the time he had reached the near shore, Captain Cockle was already walking as fast as he could up the dirt path to the farmhouse. It would be a good long walk, too. A couple of miles, at least. But thankfully he was still pretty fit and his damp clothes weren't dragging him down too much.

"Better keep to the side of the path, though," he told himself. "Because you never know what sort of wild birds and the like would spot you from the air and swoop down." He would rather be at sea in a storm any day.

From behind him came the familiar rolling boom of giant footsteps. Captain Cockle turned and pushed his way through the stiff wide blades of grass into the undergrowth at the side of the path. To his right, a gigantic rubber boot the size of a lorry crashed down on the path and a column of blue denim swept by as the boy passed him. Looking up, Captain Cockle caught a glimpse of the bright yellow hull of the *Cormorant*. He hoped William had done as he was told and strapped himself in. How were they ever going to get out of this mess?

Still, for a man who had almost sunk the *Tirpitz*, who had sailed the seven seas and even caught the Loch Ness monster, that should be no trouble at all. It was all about positive thinking. Captain Horatio Nelson Cockle RN pulled himself up to his full two inches in height, and strode purposefully up the path, marching manfully in the direction the boy had taken.

And then he stopped dead in his tracks.

The boy wasn't heading for the farmhouse at all. He had turned to the right across the lawn and strode to a wooden shed with a large glass window at the edge of the farmyard. Captain Cockle watched in horror as the boy opened the door, took the *Cormorant* inside, and emerged empty-handed. Then he shut and locked the door, turned, and skipped back to the farmhouse.

"Good Lord!" breathed Captain Cockle. "How am I ever going to get the *Cormorant* out of there?"

He looked desperately at his watch. They had a little over five hours left!

"Catherine?" he whispered into his radio. "Can you hear me?"

Dr Cockle tried to hold the heavy plastic wardrobe door shut. It was hard work because there was no handle on the inside and the thick plastic hinges were stiff, almost pulling her arms out of their sockets. Thick, rubbery clothes were crammed in behind her on rough plastic hangers and the smell of it all was making her sick.

But she dared not let the door fall open.

Outside, the whole front wall of the doll's house had been lifted away, flooding it with light. A huge hand was lifting furniture and stupid, smiling dolls in and out of the bedroom. Blondes, brunettes and redheads, with all sorts of outfits, boy dolls with vacant expressions, tables, chairs, cupboards and sofas flew through the air as Abigail played with her doll's-house.

"Who is she talking to?" hissed Jenny softly, from behind a stiff plastic mackintosh.

"I think she's just talking to her dolls," whispered Dr Cockle. "You used to do that all the time when you were her age."

"I did not!"

"Sshh! She'll hear you!"

"I did not talk to my dolls when I was . . ."

"Sshh! Listen!"

"There you are, Alice!" said Abigail, setting a blonde doll in a denim outfit on the bed with a dozen others. "You rest up there with all your friends and talk about what it's like to be rich. We were rich once, when we lived in the city, and I had lots of friends to talk to me. But we live in the country now and I don't have anyone to talk to any more. Mummy says it's because Daddy doesn't stick up for himself at work. She says he lets people take advantage of him. What do you think, Alice? Do you stick up for yourself? I bet if anyone tries to steal your things you bash them, don't you? I bet you get your friends to stick up for you."

She reached in through the open side of the doll's-house again and took one of the boy dolls from the bed.

"Do you know where my daddy's special Abigail doll is?" she asked it. "The one he said could talk. If I knew where it was, I could make us all rich again and we could afford pizza, with mushrooms and salami on the top. But Mummy says Uncle Dennis stole it. What do you think? The police couldn't find it the last time they were here and there was a terrible row. Would you like a new shirt to wear?"

And she reached for the wardrobe.

Captain Cockle was exhausted. His damp clothes clung to his body, rubbing a rash down the inside of his legs. His feet felt as if somebody had hammered them flat with a mallet and sweat was running down his forehead and into his eyes.

"I should have taken retirement more seriously," he gasped and sat down on a toadstool to rest while he looked across the lawn to the shed. It was a fine wooden shed with a plate-glass window stretching all the way along the southern side to catch the sun. Not as big as his own workshop back in Piddlecombe, but a fine, solid structure nonetheless. How the devil was he ever going to get into it? Or, more to the point, how was he ever going to get the *Cormorant* out?

After a few minutes' rest, followed by half an hour's pushing and shoving between the neck-high blades of grass on the lawn, he found himself at the base of a solid white-painted door that stretched up into the sky like an impassable barrier. Halfway up, where the eighth floor would be on an office block, was the handle of the door; and from the keyhole protruded a brass key, as long as he was tall. Captain Cockle measured the height and shuddered. Then he looked at his watch.

There were just over four hours left.

He looked down at the base of the massive door. Sure enough, there was a gap at the bottom, about an inch wide in reality, but just enough space for him to slide underneath. Without pausing a second longer, Captain Horatio Nelson Cockle ran to the door, got down on his back and slid himself beneath it, into the darkness. After a few minutes of cramped scrabbling in the dust beneath the door, he found himself standing in a shed like no other he had ever been in before. He was in a vast canyon, like a wide street between two rows of skyscrapers. To his left, a wooden chest of drawers stretched up into the air, its drawers like the floors of an office block. To his right was a system of open shelves made of a metal framework with holes at regular intervals to take the shelf brackets. The shelves were packed full of old paint tins, each the size of an oil tank, and jars with paint-brushes as tall as oak trees. And, at the top of the shelving system, on a wooden workbench behind the big glass window, was the familiar yellow hull of the *Cormorant*.

"Grandad!"

"William? Where are you?"

From the edge of the workbench, high in the air, a small black dot jutted out, followed by the tiny twig of a waving arm.

"Up here! On the workbench! And guess what? There's an electric plug on the bench opposite me! We should be able to get enough power out of it to start the *Cormorant*. Can you climb up and help?"

Captain Cockle looked up in dread at the tall, tall shelf unit.

"My dear boy," he sighed. "I have a terrible secret to tell you. One of the main reasons why I joined the submarine service in the first place, all those years ago, was because I have an awful fear of heights!"

"What is it you have to climb, Grandad?" came William's voice over the radio.

"It's a shelving unit. Like the one your grandmother has in her greenhouse for keeping her flowerpots on."

"One with little holes in the metal edges for the bolts?"

"Yes."

"Well, there's your answer, then! Stand on the inside of the shelving system and climb up the inside of the supports. That way, if you do fall it will only be a few feet on to the shelf below."

"But what about when I get to the top of each section? I'll have to climb around the outside to get to the shelf above."

"Ah . . . I'm sure you won't mind. Will you, Grandad?"

Captain Cockle peered up at the towering wall of steel, and thought about the long drop from its shelves on to the concrete floor.

"No, of course not," he said. Then he swallowed hard and started to climb.

It was all right, well, as all right as it could be, until he got to the top of the first bracket. The round screw holes, each about two feet across, were like the steps of an enormous ladder, and having the paint tins behind him made it seem as if he was in a room, which was not too bad. But, after a few minutes, his head touched the black painted ceiling of the first metal shelf and he had to twist himself around outside the shelf, out into space, to crawl up on to the next level. It was horribly frightening, and he felt that at any moment he was going to fall. The painted metal of the shelves was very smooth, even for somebody as small as himself, and fear was making his palms wet and slippery with sweat.

"Are you OK, Grandad?"

"I'm all right, William. How many more shelves are there?"

"Let me see. One . . . two . . . three . . . Ah, six, I think."

"Good Lord!" said Captain Cockle, and started to climb again. The next shelf ceiling was much worse than the one before because, by now, he was at least fifty feet up in the air. It was a long drop to the concrete floor of the shed and Captain Cockle's legs were actually starting to tremble with the strain. Captain Cockle had faced death many times before during the war and during his adventures since, but none of those times seemed as terrible as this awful fear he felt now.

"Come on, Grandad! You can do it!"

"How much further to go?"

"Only another three shelves, Grandad!"

Captain Cockle stood on the top of the third shelf bracket under the fourth shelf and squirmed his way round the outside edge, hanging out into space, at least sixty feet up from the floor. His fingers scraped the metal for a hold and his legs shuddered as he poised to push himself up.

Behind him there was a low thumping noise that grew louder and louder. Suddenly, with a ringing metallic clang, he heard the key of the shed door turn and saw the knob of the door swivel.

"William, get inside the *Cormorant* and shut the hatch!"

"Grandad!"

"Quickly now!"

A crack of light split along the edge of the door and there were the two giant children, followed by a gigantic brown-and-white monster of a dog that burst past them into the shed, charged down the space between the shelves and the chest of drawers and then turned, to stare straight up at Captain Cockle!

11

THE LITTLE PEOPLE

Captain Cockle heaved himself up over the lip of the shelf just as the dog slammed into the metal frame. He felt its hot breath on his face and the power of its jaws as they snapped shut on the shelving bracket. There was a deafening crash as the dog knocked over a dozen paint tins and sent jamjars of paint-brushes spinning and smashing on the concrete far below.

Captain Cockle rolled towards the back of the shelving, behind a huge white car battery as big as a house.

"William! Are you all right?"

"I'm fine. I'm inside the *Cormorant*. How about you?"

"I'll be fine if I can stay behind this car battery. It should be heavy enough to protect me against the brute."

The dog jumped at the shelf again, reached out

to try and get his head between the shelves and his jaws around Captain Cockle, while his paws scrabbled on the metalwork. His nose punched the solid wall of the battery and he fell back with a yelp on to the floor. But Captain Cockle's escape was short-lived. The dog had pushed the battery right up against the wall. There was no space left any more, and nowhere to hide. The dog crouched on the concrete, snarled, and jumped again. "Crash!" it went against the metal shelves. The huge slobbering jaws opened and the head reached in.

"Timmy! Stop that! We're not supposed to be in here!"

Suddenly the head was jerked backwards. An enormous arm had grabbed the collar and pulled it away from the shelving. Captain Cockle heard the giant boy's voice and there was a thundering, scuffling sound in the canyon below. Then more booming footsteps, the crash of the door closing and, for a moment, silence.

The two giant children were there in the shed with them!

"We shouldn't be in here, Sam!" whispered Abigail. "It's Daddy's workshop."

"He won't mind when he finds out what I've got," said Sam proudly. "Look!" And he pointed to the *Cormorant*, resting on his father's workbench. "See! Dad hasn't lost his touch at all. It's the new toy for Christmas this year! Better than the solar-powered aeroplane or that silly talking doll – a radio-controlled submarine! And I saved it from being washed down the weir. I bet Dad was keeping it a secret from Mum just so that he could surprise her. We'll all be rich again, Abbie, and Uncle Dennis can put that in his pipe and smoke it!"

Abigail looked at the *Cormorant* closely, peering into the portholes and poking at the mechanical arms and propellers. William kept as still as a rock. He watched Abigail's eye peering at him, and stared straight ahead.

"Humm," said Abigail. "It looks good, I suppose, and I like the little pilot inside, but I've got an even better surprise for Dad. You know how Uncle Dennis said that the talking doll never existed, and how Dad made it all up in his head? Well, look at this!" And she carefully put a plastic doll's wardrobe down on the workbench next to the *Cormorant* and opened the door with her finger.

Lying in amongst the dolls' clothes inside were Dr Cockle and Jenny. Both were standing very straight, with fixed expressions on their faces, staring straight forward. Dr Cockle was dressed in a stiff red raincoat with a huge floppy hat.

"Good Lord, Catherine!" gasped Captain Cockle as he watched from the shelves below.

"Aren't they detailed?" said Abigail, as she gently poked Jenny's T-shirt with her fingernail. "Look at the little fingers and hair. It's almost as if they're real. Look at the cross expression on the little old lady doll!"

Sam leant closer.

"Do they talk?"

"Of course!" said Abigail. "You just have to push them in their stomachs. Watch . . ."

"If you hit me in the stomach again, young lady, I'll scream!" shouted Dr Cockle, in her loudest schoolmistress voice. "And take this ridiculous coat off me at once! I can hardly move my arms!"

"Oh, they're haunted!" gasped Abigail and rushed around behind her brother.

Sam bent closer and looked carefully at Dr Cockle as she stood tapping her foot angrily on the bench and pulling back on her cardigan and coat.

"Wow!" he breathed. "Fantastic! I didn't think Dad was this good!" And he reached forward to touch Dr Cockle, who gave his finger a hard whack with her medical bag.

"I am *not* one of your father's dolls!" she insisted. "Please leave me alone!"

"Then what are you?" said Sam. "I bet you have a microprocessor inside you and run on batteries!"

Dr Cockle tried to think of a story she thought children would believe.

"I . . . I . . ." she said, looking at Abigail. "I am the queen of the fairies!"

Abigail made a face and blew a loud raspberry.

"If you're the queen of the fairies," she said,

"then show us some magic! Nobody believes in fairies any more. Not even kids!"

"All right, then!" said Dr Cockle in a huff. "I . . . I'm a leprechaun!"

"A what?" said Sam.

"You know! An Irish pixie! One of the 'Little People!'"

"If you're a leprechaun," said Abigail calmly, "then why haven't you got an Irish accent?"

"Um . . . Er . . . Because I've lived in England for a long time and lost it!" said Dr Cockle. "That's why!"

"Tell them the truth, Granny!" hissed Jenny from the wardrobe.

"Let's face it," said Sam. "Kids don't believe in fairies and leprechauns any more. If you said you were from outer space, or part of some secret government experiment, we'd probably believe you. But fairies and leprechauns . . . well, nobody thinks they're real any more!"

"Ah . . . excuse me! Down here!" shouted Captain Cockle from the shelves under the workbench, and waved his arm. Abigail stepped back in alarm.

"There's another one!" said Sam. "A little old man! Now he *looks* like a leprechaun!"

"He's my husband!" said Dr Cockle.

"Captain Horatio Nelson Cockle at your service," said Captain Cockle waving nervously. "Look . . ah . . . children. You've guessed right. We are part of an experiment . . . one of my inventions, actually . . . that went wrong. I've been working with a special machine for reducing atomic structure which is built into that submarine there on the bench, and it went off by accident. That's why we're so small and, unless we can get enough power to enlarge us back to full size in the next two hours, we're going to be stuck like this for the rest of our lives. What are your names?"

"I'm Sam Sutcliffe and this is my sister Abbie," said Sam, kneeling down so that his face was level with Captain Cockle's. "Our dad's Stephen Sutcliffe, of the Sutcliffe-Pratt toy company."

"Jolly good company," said Captain Cockle. "I've made some of their model kits. Very realistic, I must say. You've met my wife Catherine, and that is my grandson William in the *Cormorant*, and his sister Jenny there in Abigail's wardrobe. Now, can you lift me up on to the workbench and help us get the electricity we need?"

Abigail looked very sad.

"You mean you're not Daddy's talking doll and we won't be rich any more?" she said, close to tears.

"What's all this about the doll that everyone's talking about?" asked Dr Cockle from the workbench.

"Dad's a toy designer," said Sam, as he lifted Captain Cockle up from amongst the paint tins and stood him gently on the workbench. "And he's really good, too, honestly he is. It's just that, being an inventor and thinking all sorts of new thoughts all the time doesn't make him very good at practical stuff like business."

"I can imagine," said Dr Cockle, looking at her husband.

"Anyway, Dad has this friend called Dennis Pratt whom he met at college. They set up the Sutcliffe-Pratt toy company together, with Dad doing all the inventing and Dennis doing all the accounts and that. We moved down to the city as well, but Dad didn't like it, and when things started going wrong for him we moved back up here to my granddad's old farm."

"I hate it," said Abigail. "I had to leave all my friends behind and now I've nobody to play with."

"How did things go wrong for your father?" asked Captain Cockle, pacing up and down the workbench, as he always did when he was thinking hard about something.

"His ideas started getting stolen by another toy company," said Sam. "Mum says that Dennis Pratt was selling them without telling Dad and pocketing the money. But, because Uncle Dennis manages all the accounts, there's no proof."

"Mum says Uncle Dennis is a 'con man'," said Abigail. "She tried to call the police on him when the doll went missing. But nobody could prove it was him."

"And the doll was never found," added Sam. "It was a special doll that talks when you speak to it, and not prerecorded voices either, proper speech. It was all done with a miniature computer, and it went missing on the day that Uncle Dennis came here to go over the company accounts with Dad."

"Couldn't your father build another?" asked Captain Cockle.

"The computer disc with all the plans on it and the spare microprocessor all went missing at the same time – it was worth a lot of money, you see. It would have made Dad rich and put his company back on its feet."

Dr Cockle made a loud "tut-tutting" sound. "Surely the police must have some idea where it went," she said.

"They searched the shed, and the bushes, and the house," said Sam. "And most of all they searched Uncle Dennis, and his car. He was furious. But they couldn't find it anywhere. It broke Dad's heart. He hasn't invented anything good since. When I picked your submarine out of the pond, I thought it was a new toy Dad had made, and I was so happy for him. Abigail thought that your wife was another talking doll. But she's not, is she? And now we won't have any money and Mum and Dad will never be happy again. You should see the way they fight about it!"

Captain Cockle's pacing had taken him over to the big plate-glass window behind the workbench. He was looking across the lawn and down the footpath to the pond. For a long while he stared out at the water, where the *Cormorant* had crashed and sunk to the bottom, and . . .

"Did you ever see this 'Uncle Dennis' of yours with a brief-case?" he said suddenly. "A flat black one?"

"Not lately," said Sam. "But he used to have one that Dad gave him."

"Was it flat and black?"

Suddenly Dr Cockle, Jenny and William knew where the doll had gone. Captain Cockle did too, because he said, "How about a swap? If you and Abigail help us get enough power from the socket here in the shed, so that we can fly up to those pylons at the end of the field and get the really big charge of electricity we need to work our miniaturiser, I'll find that doll for you and your father can be rich again."

"And we can go back to the city and never have to eat rotten old pike again!" laughed Abigail.

"Exactly!" smiled Captain Cockle. "Now William, you grab the laptop computer from the control room and we'll have young Sam here take you and Rover out on the pond. Catherine, you and Jenny stay here with Abigail and we'll have a go at rigging up a power line to reach that socket over there. Hurry now, because we have just over an hour and a half left!"

12

SALVAGE OPERATIONS

Five minutes later, William felt as if he was flying through the air – wedged tight inside the top pocket of Sam's lumberjack shirt, gripping the coarse material as the wind whipped at his hair and the footpath shot past hundreds of feet below.

"Whatever you do, don't trip!" he shouted, but he didn't think that Sam could hear him. Sam was only interested in recovering the brief-case and proving his father had been telling the truth about the doll. That suited William, too, because the faster they could recover the doll, the faster they could get power for the *Cormorant* and enlarge back to full size. Being less than two inches tall was quite exciting for a while, but William did not want to stay that way for the rest of his life. What would his mother say . . . ?

Beside him in the pocket was Rover, still smelling very fishy from its time in the pike's stomach, and a black padded satchel containing one of the laptop computers from the *Cormorant*. With these and Rover's joypad control, William had all he needed to mount his own one-man salvage operation. He watched as the end of the footpath shot towards them and there, off to the left and hidden in the reeds, was a small rowing-boat.

"Are you all right down there?" whispered Sam, and William could feel the words vibrate through Sam's chest as he spoke.

"I'm fine!" he shouted. "Put me down on the seat of the boat, and I can be setting up Rover as we go." He looked at his watch. There was just under an hour and a quarter to the deadline.

"The ones marked with a cross are suitable for recharging and the others are burnt out," said Captain Cockle. "All you have to do is slot them back into the spaces on the battery board with the positive ends towards the bow and the negative ends towards the stern."

Dr Cockle stared at the rows and rows of little batteries that lined the battery room floor.

"There must be hundreds of them!" she said.

"Four hundred and thirty-six live ones, to be precise," said Captain Cockle. "William and I had to take them all out and test them this morning, together with the three hundred and sixty-four dead ones that were damaged by the lightning strike. You slot these in and I'll go and direct Abigail and Jenny with the wires."

Captain Cockle ran back into the engine-room, and lifted the hatch leading to the diving room. Below him, Jenny was pulling a heavy white double cable through the open airlock door. The ends of it looked as if they had been chewed up by a large animal, with about two feet of thick copper metal showing through.

"Abigail's finding it difficult to cut off the plastic," said Jenny.

"I'll go and see if I can help. Can you manage?"

Jenny lugged at the heavy cable, sliding more of it into the submarine from outside.

"Yes, I can manage, Granddad. Where do you want me to connect it?"

"Pull it up through this hatch here and bring it into the battery compartment where your grandmother is. I'll come back in a minute and secure it to the main input grid. Then all we have to do is switch on."

He climbed back up the metal ladder and out of the conning tower hatch on to the deck. Between the two benches, Abigail was frowning in concentration as she tried to follow Captain Cockle's instructions.

"I keep cutting right though the wire!" she moaned. "I've done it three times already and it won't work! Daddy never lets us do this. He says it's dangerous to play with electricity!"

"And he's absolutely right!" said Captain Cockle, trying not to look at his watch. "Rest the wire on the edge of the bench and just roll it gently under the knife blade. There! You have it! Now, very carefully, put the blade under the cut and pull it towards you . . . gently now . . . gently!"

The white plastic coating slipped back, revealing three inches of gleaming copper wire. Abigail smiled proudly.

"Jolly good!" said Captain Cockle. "Now all you have to do is to uncover the other wire and then we're all set to plug it in. Make sure your hands are well clear of the wires when you do!"

Out on the pond, William was standing on a fishing-tackle box and peering out over the side of the boat into the water looking for the radio buoy. It seemed ages ago since he had been trapped down there in the dark water, and it was hard to think just how far they had been from the shore when they had crashed. He looked back to get his bearings on the footpath and the house. Then he flicked a switch on Rover's joypad and held it out over the side.

"What are you doing?" said Sam.

"Looking for an orange radio buoy. It marks the spot where we crashed."

"How big is it?"

"About the size of a football . . . ah . . . for me, that is. For you, it'll only be about the size of . . . um . . . a peanut!"

Sam screwed up his eyes and stared hard at the water.

"How will we ever see it?"

"There's a radio tracker in this joypad control. Granny and Jenny used it to track Rover when he was lost in that fish's stomach, so it'll probably work here too. The radio transmitter in the buoy is much more powerful than Rover's homing device." And he plugged a set of headphones into the joypad so that he could hear the signal better.

The screeching roar of the radio nearly made him fall off the tackle box.

"We must be right on top of it! We must have floated over it without seeing it!"

"Hang on," said Sam. "I'll row back a bit. You watch and see if it floats out from under the boat."

"Just take your time, Abigail," shouted Captain Cockle from the conning tower of the *Cormorant*. "You're pressing too hard with the knife."

Abigail was getting flustered. She only had one more wire to go but, as hard as she tried, the more she kept cutting right through it when she only wanted to cut off the plastic covering. Little sections of wire and plastic coating littered the workbench and Abigail was getting more and more cross.

"Just lay the wire on the bench and roll the blade gently on top of it," coaxed Captain Cockle. "Gently now . . . there! Now, carefully pull off the covering."

Abigail slid the knife blade forward, and two inches of gleaming copper wire showed itself from beneath the plastic coat. Abigail smiled proudly again.

"There," said Captain Cockle. "We'll make an electrician out of you yet!"

"But I want to be a dress designer," said Abigail.

"Whatever, my dear. Now, you wait there while I go below and see how we're getting on here."

Down below in the battery room, Jenny had hauled up the other end of the wire and was standing with the two bare ends in her hands.

"Jolly good!" said Captain Cockle. "Now, let's see about securing those to the main input grid. Pass me a screwdriver, Jenny, and we'll have that done in a flash. How are you getting on, Catherine?"

"Four hundred and thirty-four, four hundred and thirty-five, four hundred and thirty-six!" announced Dr Cockle triumphantly as she slotted the last battery in place. "How much longer have we got?"

"An hour and ten minutes . . . "

"This is cutting it very fine. I hope William is all right!"

"There it is!" said Sam, pointing down over the side of the boat to where a tiny orange ball floated on the surface. He reached over to grab it.

"Don't!" yelled William. "You'll pull the anchor up off the bottom and then we'll never be able to tell where the brief-case is. Have you got any strong fishing-line in this tackle box of yours?"

"I don't know, but we have this. Will it do?" And he picked up his father's fishing-rod from the seat of the boat.

"Great!" said William. "We can cut the hook off and use the line!"

Very carefully, and as delicately as if he was threading line into the eye of a fish-hook, Sam fiddled the cut end of the fishing-line through Rover's propeller guard and tied it tight. Then he paid out line from the reel and, holding the rod in one hand, lifted the tiny submersible, which was only the size of a pill in the palm of his hand, and laid it gently in the water next to the orange radio buoy.

"There," he said. "All set!"

William was sitting on the tackle box with the joypad in his hands and the laptop computer open so that he could see the screen. On it was a wobbling picture from Rover's camera. It showed the bottom of the boat stretching into the distance like the underside of a huge supertanker. Then it dipped down into the dark water of the pond, following the anchor line of the radio buoy towards the bottom.

Sam carefully paid out more line as Rover dived.

"If anyone sees us they'll think we're fishing," he said.

"They'll think *you're* fishing," said William. "They won't see me at all!"

"Anything on the camera yet?"

William peered at the laptop computer screen. Even with powerful lights to guide him, it was difficult to see where Rover was. Then out of the fog, came a strange plant, like a giant palm tree. William guided Rover down its stem, and there were more of them. Big thick weeds, just like the ones that had been wrapped around the *Cormorant*'s rotor blades, and then . . .

There was the big, square slab of the brief-case, sitting fair and square on the bottom of the pond. William could see where the *Cormorant* had brushed the mud off it and over to the side was the dark crescent of the handle.

"I have it!" said William. "It's right under us!"

"Uncle Dennis must have thrown it into the pond when he thought he was going to get caught with my dad's doll inside it!" snorted Sam angrily. "Nobody thought of looking here, because nobody thought that anyone would throw away something as valuable as the doll. How are we going to get it up again? It's too deep to reach with the landing-net . . ."

"Just pay out some more line until I tell you to stop," said William and, with his eyes on the screen and his fingers on the joypad control buttons, he guided Rover down over the flat, black skin of the brief-case, across the edge and down towards the black curve of the handle.

"Gently does it!" he breathed, as the gap between the handle and the case seemed to yawn open and swallow the screen. Then he turned the little submersible around and headed for the silvery mirror of the surface, watching for the dark hull of the boat and the long thin curve of Sam's fishing-rod.

"Keep paying out line, Sam! We're almost there!"

With a "plop" that only William could hear, Rover broke the surface, trailing the fishing-line with it. Sam reached over with the landing-net and brought the little submersible aboard, undid the nylon and tied it to the seat. Then, with William watching carefully, he gently hauled on the fishing reel. The line went taut as it took the strain on the brief-case. The rod bent over as if Sam were landing a monster fish. The boat listed over in the water.

"Will the line break?" shouted William.

"It shouldn't. We've . . ."

Suddenly, the boat rocked back as the line jerked and went slack.

"Oh no! It's broken . . ."

"No, it hasn't. Look!"

The line went tight again and began to sway, as if something heavy was swinging at the end of it.

"We just pulled the case out of the mud. Haul away now! We have it!"

Sam carefully reeled in the line, while William watched the water. Deep in the pond, a dark shape appeared, trailing clouds of mud. As it broke the surface, Sam reached over with the landing-net and, putting down the rod, hauled in the briefcase. Muddy water spurted all over the seat and over Sam's jeans. William had to hide behind the tackle box to avoid getting splattered.

There was a loud thud, and there on the seat was the missing brief-case. It was covered in thick black mud, but around the lock the water had washed some of it away and it was easy to read the gold initials.

"DP."

"Dennis Pratt!" snorted Sam, and reached forward to undo the catches. "It's locked!"

"Your dad has tools in his shed," said William, and they both looked back towards the shore.

There, at the top of the footpath near the farmhouse, an old Volvo estate car was drawing up. Sam's father got out of it. He was looking towards the pond.

"He's seen us!" said Sam.

"Who's that?" asked William.

Getting out of the car on the passenger side was a smaller man in a very expensive raincoat. He turned towards the pond and looked where Sam's father was pointing. He suddenly appeared very cross.

"Oh, no," said Sam softly. "It's Dennis Pratt!"

"Right then," said Captain Cockle. "We have the power line connected up to the socket on the other bench, we have the wire connected to the input grid and we have all the batteries that can be used in place. Catherine, you go and stand on the bench so that you can signal Abigail to switch on the power when I say. Jenny, you go up into the control room and monitor the power level. I'll stay here and check that the electricity doesn't trip the fuses. All keep in touch by radio, understood?"

"Aye, aye, Grandad," said Jenny.

"Yes, Horatio," said Dr Cockle. "We have less than an hour left, you know." And she climbed down the diving chamber ladder, out past the wires stretching though the open airlock hatch and on to the bench outside. The wires reached across the bench over to the far workbench and coiled around the pins of a plug connected to a desk lamp. In the gap between the two benches, Abigail stood with her finger resting on the switch next to the plug.

Captain Cockle checked that everyone was in place and that the connection from the wire to the *Cormorant* was firm. Then he stood away from any bare metal – just in case – and said, "Right, Catherine, switch it on!"

Dr Cockle waved to Abigail. Abigail pressed the switch.

And nothing happened.

"Have you turned on the power yet, Granny?" asked Jenny from the control room.

"The lamp that the wire's plugged into has come on!" said Dr Cockle. "Why isn't the power reaching the batteries?"

"Are you sure you put all the batteries in the right way round, Catherine?"

"I did the best I could, Horatio!" said Dr Cockle stiffly. "Given that there were over four hundred of them and we were rushed for time. I don't understand why you couldn't invent just one or two big batteries rather than all those little ones, if you're going to make such a fuss about it!"

Captain Cockle ran his eyes over the four hundred and thirty-six batteries. It was like trying to see which bulb in a string of Christmas tree lights was broken. Then he saw one the wrong way round, and another, and another. Quickly, after Abigail had turned the power off, he turned the batteries round, checked as best he could that they were all in correctly, and shouted into his microphone.

"All right, Catherine. Tell Abigail to switch on again!"

Dr Cockle raised her hand to Abigail but, before Abigail's finger could push down the switch, the door of the shed burst open and Sam rushed in with a muddy brief-case in his hand and his clothes all covered in dirt.

"Quick, Abbie!" he hissed. "Hide the Cockles! Dad and Uncle Dennis are right behind me. We can't let them in!"

Dr Cockle turned to climb back up into the diving chamber but, before she could run back across the bench to the *Cormorant*, she saw four huge fingers surround her, trap her, and whisk her off her feet. Her stomach churned as she was swung high in the air, twisted sideways, and dropped into a gigantic sack that seemed as if it was strapped to some huge animal. The sack shook and rocked. There was a thunderous slam behind her as the shed door closed and the sack seemed to calm down – heaving and falling with the breath of some mighty animal. Outside the sack, she heard heavy, grown-up giant footsteps coming closer. Then they stopped, and Abigail's father said, "And what have you two been doing?"

"What happened, Horatio?" she breathed into her radio microphone.

"Abigail's father came back," said Captain Cockle. "Abigail panicked and put you in her top pocket. She's gone outside and I can't see where you are. Did Abigail switch on the power?"

Dr Cockle tugged at the fabric of Abigail's shirt, trying to pull herself upright in the pocket.

"I don't think so."

"What are we going to do? We only have forty-five minutes left! Where's William?"

"Over here in Sam's pocket, Grandad! We're both outside!"

Dr Cockle's head pushed against a heavy flap of

fabric. It was a button-down pocket, and Abigail had it buttoned down. In the very corner was a gap, just big enough for Dr Cockle to look through. Very gingerly, she prised open the gap and peered out.

Stephen Sutcliffe was towering above her, talking to Sam and Abigail. He did not seem very pleased. Standing next to him was a smaller man, with dark slicked-back hair and twinkly brown eyes. The sides of his face were bluey-black, as if he had been travelling for a long time and had not shaved.

He was looking at the mud on Sam's clothes with a worried expression, and kept casting glances back towards the pond.

"How many times have I told you, Sam, not to go out on the pond fishing in the boat by yourself? You might have tipped it up and drowned. And I suppose you were using my fishing-rod too, the only one we have now?"

"Yes, Dad, but . . ."

"And you, Abigail, I've told you that my workshop is out of bounds to you children. It should have been locked. Here!" And Mr Sutcliffe leant past the two children with a key and turned it in the lock.

"But, Dad!" said Sam.

"What?"

Sam looked at Abigail. She looked back.

"Ah . . . nothing."

"And why are your clothes all covered with mud?"

Dr Cockle could see Dennis Pratt prick up his ears at this.

"I was just messing in the water."

"Hunting for buried treasure?" said Dennis Pratt. He obviously meant to make a joke of it, but Dr Cockle could hear the hard edge in his voice.

"No. I was just messing."

Stephen Sutcliffe slipped the key to the shed into his pocket. Four pairs of eyes, two large and two small, watched it disappear from sight.

"I want you to come up to the house," he said. "Uncle Dennis has come to make a business proposition to me and it concerns the whole family. I want you to be there to hear what he has to say."

"Can't we stay here?" said Sam.

His father's voice was firm.

"No," he said. "This concerns everyone."

"I'm sorry," whispered Sam towards his shirt pocket.

"I should hope so," said his father. "Your mother is going to have a terrible job trying to get the mud out of those clothes now that the washing-machine is broken."

"We're going back to the house, Horatio," hissed Dr Cockle into her radio microphone. "And the father's locked the shed door. Do you have any power in the batteries?"

"Hardly enough to boil an egg, my dear! And

I'm on the wrong side of the shed to switch on the wire from the socket. Our only hope is to tell the adults what is going on and hope they understand."

"What about this Pratt person? If he stole Mr Sutcliffe's secrets, what might he do with something as big as your miniaturiser!"

"Well, we have to do something, dear, and fast. We only have forty minutes left!"

13

DESPERATE MEASURES

Captain Cockle ran up into the control room and looked across Jenny's shoulder at the power gauges. There was a small flicker of life in one of the reserve systems.

"We certainly don't have enough electricity to get us airborne," he said, looking at the computer screen. "But we might have enough power to use the mechanical arms and the electric winch for a few minutes. Jenny, how far do you think the gap is between this bench and the one where the power supply is?"

"About a metre, Grandad."

"And how long is . . . that piece of curtain rail on the bench over there?"

"I don't know. But I'd say it would just about reach across the gap."

"Right, then. The curtain rod is too heavy for either of us to lift on our own, but with the mechanical arms we may stand a chance. Now, let's see. You were always better at this than I was. See if you can make us a bridge."

Captain Cockle swung over the two telescopic controls, and the metal gloves that controlled the powerful mechanical arms stowed on the underside of the *Cormorant*'s nose, and passed them to Jenny. There was a "click" and a weak watery "whirr" and two yellow metal claws on the end of long silvery arms reached out from beneath the portholes along the top of the bench. Captain Cockle could feel what was left of the power draining away. With a soft click, first one and then the other claw fastened on to the end of the plastic curtain rail, twisted it round and balanced it upright on the edge of the bench, Jenny struggled to tip the rail over before all the power was gone.

"Well done! Here we go," breathed Captain Cockle, as Jenny let the curtain rail fall.

For a sickening moment, Jenny thought the curtain rail was going to fall short and tumble into the chasm. Then she saw it hit the opposite bench, bounce once, twice, and then come to rest in place with a loud clatter, as a shaky bridge between the two benches.

Suddenly, from outside the shed came a ferocious bark and a deafening thud as Tim hurled himself at the door.

"It's that blasted dog again!" said Captain Cockle. "He must have heard the noise when the curtain rail fell in place. Well, at least Sam's father locked the door after them. Now, let's go and see how safe that bridge is. I wish your grandmother were here now, she has a far better head for heights that I ever did."

"The reason Dennis asked to come up here today," said Stephen Sutcliffe, "is to talk about the way things are going in our toy business and to tell us what we can do to help. And, since any decision we might have to make will include the whole family, I thought it would be better to have you all here."

They were all sitting around the big wooden dining-table in the kitchen. From where she was trapped in Abigail's top pocket Dr Cockle could see the cooker where she and Jenny had been trapped earlier in the afternoon, and the doll's-house where Abigail had found them. It all seemed so different from up here, when you didn't have to worry about dogs, or cats, or people stepping on your head.

The people looked different, too. Mr Sutcliffe looked tired, as if he had fought a long battle and lost. Young Sam looked as if he was close to tears, and his mother Mary looked just plain angry. She kept looking daggers at Dennis Pratt, who had taken off his coat to reveal a very dapper business suit. He had a leather folder with lots of papers in it. There were columns and rows of figures, and what looked like some kind of contract, but Dr

Cockle, as a proper lady of integrity, had never taught herself to read other people's papers upside down.

"Well, thank you, Stephen," said Dennis Pratt. "And thank you, Mary, Sam, and dear Abbie for letting me come and explain things to you all." He had a very oily voice, the sort of voice that Dr Cockle remembered her fishmonger put on when he tried to tell her all his fish was freshly caught and thought she couldn't tell the difference. "You see, the Sutcliffe-Pratt toy company has had to fight an uphill battle against a lot of other toy companies in the past few years, toy companies which, may I say, have more money for research into new toys and more money for advertising them on television. This has meant that, to beat these companies, we have had to keep coming up with new toys that are better and cheaper than those the other companies make."

"Stephen did . . ." began Mary, but her husband put his hand on her arm. She glowered at him, and then at Dennis Pratt.

"That's right, Mary," continued Dennis. "Stephen did. We had the stringless puppets, and the three-dimensional snakes and ladders, and lots of great ideas. But that was in the past, when Stephen was not . . . how shall I say it . . . under so much stress!"

"You put him under stress," said Mary. "I will

not have you sit here and tell our children lies about their father when we all know that . . ."

"Mary, please," said Stephen.

"Mary," said Dennis Pratt. "I'm as sad to see the toy company in trouble as much as anyone. It's my life as well as Stephen's. We built it up together. But now we are in so much debt, because Stephen cannot seem to come up with good ideas any more that I'm afraid we need to raise cash fast if the company is to survive. I've agreed to put up my life savings, and I've come here to ask you and the family if you can raise some money by selling this house . . ."

Back in the shed, Captain Cockle was standing with his left foot on the white plastic of the curtain rail and the right foot on the bench, staring into space. Around his middle, as a safety measure, was a long piece of elastic thread from one of the dolls on the workbench, and on his face was the sort of expression people have going for major root canal work at the dentist's. He could feel his legs shaking and the sweat breaking out on his forehead. In front of him, the whole workshop seemed to sway sickeningly.

"Are you all right, Grandad?" called Jenny from the control room.

"Just a slight problem with the . . . ah . . . altitude," stammered Captain Cockle.

He lifted his right foot off the bench and . . . put

it back. Then he tried again. Up came the foot on to the curtain rail. It seemed very, very thin! The world moved again . . . and back went the foot on to the bench.

"Ah . . . Jenny," groaned Captain Cockle. "I have a . . . er . . . a confession to make."

"About being scared of heights?" asked Jenny. "Granny told me about that years ago. She said it was the main reason you joined the submarine service. Would you like me to go across? We do that sort of thing in gymnastics every week at school. There's no use trying to pretend, you know."

"Women!" muttered Captain Cockle to himself. "Ah . . . yes, Jenny. If you wouldn't mind."

"You can't sell this house!" cried Mary. "It's been in Stephen's family for generations. He was born here and so was his father, and his father before him."

"I know that, Mary," said Dennis. "And believe me, if things weren't so desperate I wouldn't be asking you now. But if you sell the house and put the money with mine, we'll have enough to pay off the company debts and start afresh. You and Stephen might be able to buy it back in a few years."

"I don't believe you," snapped Mary. "It was you that got us into this mess in the first place!"

A slightly threatening tone came into Dennis Pratt's voice just then.

"Now, Mary, you remember what happened the last time you made silly accusations like that . . ."

"The only problem the last two times was that you covered up the proof," said Mary. "When you stole the idea for that solar-powered aeroplane and sold it, you were clever enough to change it ever so slightly so nobody could prove it was Stephen's!"

"Now, steady on there, Mary," said Pratt. "That idea wasn't worth much, anyway. I mean, who would want a toy plane that runs on sunlight when it rains so much over here?"

"That was a good idea!" said Sam suddenly. "I liked it. It was one of Dad's best!"

"You stay out of this, please, Sam," said his father. "Dennis is right. Perhaps it wasn't such a good idea, after all."

"But it was," said Sam. "It . . ."

"And what about the doll!" said Mary, wagging her finger across the table at Pratt. "You stole that doll and the computer discs so you could sell them . . . !"

Dennis Pratt shot to his feet and glowered at Mary.

"For the last time," he shouted, "I don't know anything about a doll! I simply came up here to show Stephen the figures for the company. And the next thing I know is that you've called the police to search me and my car for some doll that never existed. I think you just invented the idea of a doll to make me think that your husband still has good ideas."

"There was, too, a doll!" said Abigail softly. "We can prove it!"

Every eye in the room turned to look at her.

Dennis Pratt seemed slightly shaken. He turned to Abigail and said slowly, "Now Abbie, I'm not talking about one of the dollies you play with in your doll's-house. I'm talking about a new dolly that your father says talks. Now, where have you ever seen a doll like that?"

Sam looked at his father, and his mother, and then at Dennis Pratt.

"In your brief-case," he said. "The one you threw into the pond."

Jenny stood on the edge of the bench with the elastic cord around her middle and the curtain rail bridge in front of her. It wasn't too frightening really, because the curtain rail, laid on its side, was a good three feet wide.

But it was a terrible drop to the floor!

"Just keep looking straight ahead and use your arms to balance, the way tightrope walkers do and . . . er . . . don't look down!" said Captain Cockle, trying to be helpful.

"I know what I'm doing," said Jenny, stepping out on to the white plastic of the curtain rail. It was slippier than she had first thought and, now she was standing on it above that awful drop, it did not seem nearly so wide either. She took a step forward, and another, trying to keep her eyes fixed on the socket in the far wall. Another step, and then another. Was she in the centre of the rail, or was she wandering to one side? Her eyes went down to her feet, and below her was the terrifying chasm.

"Oh!"

"Keep looking forward, Jenny!"

The next step was difficult to take. She didn't want to move her foot off the rail. In fact, what she really wanted to do was to get down on all fours and crawl the rest of the way, but there wasn't time.

Another step.

And then another.

She could feel the plastic curtain rail sagging under her weight now. It was bowing in the middle and starting to spring slightly with every step she took.

"That's it, Jenny. Gently does it!"

Captain Cockle had paid out a long piece of elastic now and it hung behind Jenny, pulling her to one side. It was heavier than she had first thought. Could she manage the weight all the way to the other bench?

Suddenly there was a loud bark from the other side of the shed door. Jenny jumped and almost lost her balance, wobbling unsteadily on the springy curtain rail. She felt the weight of the elastic, the slipperiness of the rail and the long, long drop below. She dropped to her knees to keep her balance and held on to the sides of the curtain rail with her hands.

"It's all right, Jenny! It's only the dog outside. He can't get in. Just stay calm."

The dog barked again, and again. Jenny breathed a sigh of relief and crawled slowly across the huge chasm to the other side. Captain Cockle looked at his watch. They had only twenty minutes left!

Dennis Pratt was *really* shaken now. He smiled at Sam in the same way that grown-ups smile at children who say they've seen fairies at the bottom of the garden.

"But I don't have a brief-case, Sam. And if I did, I certainly wouldn't throw it into a pond in your garden, now would I?"

Sam looked Dennis Pratt in the eye.

"You had a brief-case once," he said. "The one Dad gave you when you set up your company. It's made of black leather and it has your initials on it. I've seen it!"

"You probably saw it years ago," said Dennis Pratt.

"We saw it today," said Abigail. "Sam pulled it out of the pond and we hid it in your shed."

"So that's where you threw it, Dennis!" said Stephen, snapping out of the trance he was in. "The one place we didn't look. Right! Sam and Abigail, you come with me. We're going to get to the bottom of this." And, grabbing his children by the arms, he pushed past Dennis Pratt and set off across the lawn in the growing darkness with Mary, heading for the shed.

"I can't move it, Grandad! It's too stiff!"

Jenny was pulling desperately down on the big switch next to the power socket. It had never occurred to her grandfather or herself that what is simple for a fully-grown person to do might be impossible for someone who is less than two inches tall – and pushing down a fully-sized electrical switch was one of those things.

"Find something to lever it down with!" suggested Captain Cockle. "A screwdriver, or a pen, or a nail-file, or . . . anything!"

"Horatio! Can you hear me?"

"What is it, Catherine?"

"Young Sam has told his father about the brief-case. They're all coming down to the shed to have a look at it!"

"Hell's bells!" said Captain Cockle, looking at the control panel. "And we still don't have any power! Jenny! Forget the switch and get back over here. They're all going to come crashing through that door at any minute and I don't want you out there where that dog can get you!"

"But, Grandad! We don't have any electricity!"

"I know. Just get back here!"

Jenny looked at the huge switch and the wires leading to the *Cormorant*. If only she could have got the switch working!

"Come on, Jenny! They're almost here!"

Jenny glanced at the switch one last time and then ran back to the curtain rail, stepped up on to it, and started to walk gingerly back across, keeping her eyes straight ahead on the yellow hull of the *Cormorant*. She could see her grandfather beckoning to her to hurry, and in the distance she could hear the pounding of giant footsteps coming closer and closer to the door.

She was ten feet from the far bench when the shed door burst in, hit the curtain rail with a massive thump and sent her flying out into space, towards the cold hard concrete floor, a hundred feet below!

14

THE GREAT ESCAPE

Captain Cockle saw the shed door fly open and Stephen Sutcliffe come barrelling in. He saw Jenny topple and fall from the curtain rail as it clattered down into the chasm between the two benches.

"Jenny!"

Jenny screamed as the curtain rail was knocked from under her and she went flying into space. She had the most sickening feeling of falling, and saw the most horrible jumble of pictures flash past her . . . the window . . . the workbenches . . . and the shelves, spinning around her as she fell. The flat expanse of the concrete floor rushed up to meet her.

Then, all at once she felt a giant squeeze around her middle and a jerk that almost broke her spine in two as the elastic thread gripped around her waist. The concrete floor seemed to slow down in its race to meet her, stop, and then fall away again as she was jerked back up, and down, and up again.

"Jenny! Are you all right?" called Captain Cockle

134

into his radio microphone. He could see Stephen Sutcliffe looking around his workshop. He might spot Jenny at any moment.

Jenny was bouncing on the end of her bungee, with the elastic squeezing her on every bounce.

"Whoop! I'm all right, Grandad. Whoop! Can you pull me up, quick? Whoop!"

Stephen Sutcliffe had seen the *Cormorant*, he was reaching down towards it. There was no way that Captain Cockle could pull Jenny up without being seen, and no way that Stephen would miss seeing her if he didn't.

"What on earth's this . . . ?" said Stephen.

Sam was right behind him, followed by Abigail.

"I thought you'd made it, Dad. I found it . . ." he began, and then he saw Jenny, bouncing up and down below the bench. "Abbie . . . !"

Abigail rushed forward, scooped up Jenny and cupped her in her hands.

"I'll look at it later!" said Stephen, "Where's this brief-case?" and he reached back his hand to the light switch where the power lead to the *Cormorant* was attached. Without needing to look, he clicked it on!

In the darkened cabin of the *Cormorant*, Captain Cockle suddenly saw the main control panel light up like a Christmas tree as the power came back on, the main cabin lights blazed and there was a whine from deep inside the engine-room as the main motor came to life.

"Bingo!" he breathed. "We have power. Now all

we need are five minutes to recharge the batteries and we can fly!"

"We only have ten minutes left, Horatio!" hissed Dr Cockle over the radio from Abigail's top pocket. "And we're still stuck over here!"

"Did you say something, Abbie?" said Stephen.

"No, Dad!" replied Abigail, holding her cupped hands, with Jenny in them, behind her back.

"Where's this brief-case, then?"

"Here!" said Sam, and reached under the bench beneath the *Cormorant*. When he stood back up, the muddy black brief-case was in his hand.

"That looks very much like the one I gave you when we set up the company, Dennis," said Stephen sternly. "What do you think, Dennis?"

Dennis Pratt had pushed into the shed behind the Sutcliffes. He was stretching over Mary's shoulder to see what was going on.

"Ah . . . I don't know. It doesn't look like mine!"

"Put it on the bench, Sam, and let's have a look inside!"

"It's locked, Dad."

"If it's Dennis's brief-case, he'll know the combination," said Mary.

"I . . . I don't think it's mine at all," stammered Dennis.

Stephen looked at the lock, and then wiped the mud away from the brass trimming.

"But these are your initials," he said slowly. "'DP.' That's you, isn't it?"

Dennis Pratt swallowed hard. Then he said, "Look, Stephen, I didn't want to say this before when the police were here, or in front of you, Mary, but my brief-case was stolen that last time I was here. It . . . it just vanished from my car. And I did see young Sam here with it, running down to the pond. Now, I didn't want to make a fuss, but that's what happened; and if you think about it, that's the only way Sam would have known where it was."

"But Dad, I never . . ."

Stephen Sutcliffe turned slowly to face Dennis Pratt.

"If you think for one moment that I'm going to believe you after what's just happened, then you are very much mistaken," he said through clenched teeth. "I think there's only one way we can sort this out now. Mary, go and call the police!"

Mary Sutcliffe turned to run back to the house, and suddenly Dennis Pratt went wild. He grabbed at her dress and, when she broke free and ran, he swung round and made a lunge for the brief-case, pulling it off the bench and sending both Sam and Abigail tumbling to the floor.

In the control cabin, Captain Cockle heard a loud clatter, felt the *Cormorant* rock sickeningly from side to side, and suddenly the control panel dimmed as the power cable was torn from the plug on the other side of the workshop.

"Catherine! Jenny! William! Are you all right?"

Upside down in Abigail's pocket, Dr Cockle called out, "I'm fine, Horatio! What about the children?"

Jenny had untied the elastic from around her waist and was peering through Abigail's fingers at William, who was staring out of Sam's top pocket as he lay on his back on the workshop floor. Above him, Dennis Pratt and his father were struggling over the brief-case, crashing into the benches, sending paint tins flying and rocking the bench on which the *Cormorant* stood. There was a splintering smash as the desk lamp fell to the floor. Dennis Pratt grabbed it with his free hand to use as a club on Stephen's head, but Stephen already had the piece of curtain rail in his hand and jabbed it forward into Dennis's face, making him howl and fall backwards out of the shed door, taking the brief-case with him. Stephen dived after him, and the two men rolled and wrestled on the grass outside.

Sam and Abigail watched as first their father and then Dennis Pratt got the upper hand. Dennis was stronger, but Stephen was faster and taller, dodging the other man's blows and ducking under his guard.

Captain Cockle pulled himself into the pilot's seat of the *Cormorant*. On the screen in front of him, glowing in a dull green light, was the warning – "Medical Emergency 571 – Vehicle and crew have five minutes to re-enlarge! Power level 10% and falling. Repeat . . ."

"Oh, my goodness!" breathed Captain Cockle and looked at the width of the shed door. The *Cormorant* would never make it through there. The rotors would catch in the door frame and they would come crashing down.

"Catherine! Jenny! William!" he called over the radio. "Get the children to put you back up here and take the *Cormorant* outside! We've got to get going!"

In the shaking space between Abigail's fingers, Jenny kicked and shouted until Abigail held her up to her face and opened her hand.

"Quick!" she shouted into Abigail's astonished face, "You've got to let us back in our submarine. We only have a few minutes left!"

"But Daddy and Uncle Dennis are fighting!" she cried.

"Please!" shouted Jenny. "Pleeaase!"

Abigail turned and dropped Jenny roughly on the bench, scooped out Dr Cockle and dumped her there as well, and then ran outside.

"Come back and carry us through the door!" yelled Captain Cockle. But Abigail and Sam had dashed outside to help their father.

In Sam's top pocket, William shouted and kicked against the heavy material. He could feel Sam breathing heavily now and knew there was a fight going on. He heard his grandfather call over the radio, and knew that unless the *Cormorant* could reach the power cables within the next few minutes they would be trapped as miniature people forever. He pulled himself upright, grabbed the top of Sam's pocket and stuck out his head.

"Sam! Sam! You've got to help us! Take me back into the shed and bring the *Cormorant* out!"

Above him, Sam was breathing hard and crying.

"I can't!" he gasped. "My dad!"

In the light pouring out of the shed window, William could see a great battle going on. Stephen was on top of Dennis Pratt, but Dennis suddenly brought the sharp edge of the brief-case up into his opponent's face with a thud. Stephen fell backwards and toppled on to the grass. Dennis rose to his feet, held the brief-case up with both hands and aimed it at the back of Stephen's head.

"Hold it right where you are!"

At the far edge of the pool of light, Mary Sutcliffe was walking forwards with an old double-barrelled shotgun in her hand. It was pointed right at Dennis Pratt. He glanced at her and froze like a statue, with the brief-case still held up.

"Now Mary, I know we've had our differences in the past, but we can make a new start."

"Don't even speak to me, you worm! I've called the police and they'll be here in a few minutes. Now, just put that brief-case down slowly or I'll . . ."

Dennis Pratt had turned to face her, as if he was ready to do as she asked. Mary Sutcliffe saw that he was beaten and started to lower the shotgun. Then Pratt saw his chance and hurled the brief-case at her, hitting her in the chest and sending her flying backwards. There was the roar of an explosion as one of the shotgun barrels went off, and a full load of lead shot hit the big window of the shed, shattering it into a million fragments.

Dr Cockle and Jenny had just pulled themselves up into the control room when there was a terrible roaring crash as the window blasted in. Shards of razor-sharp glass smashed and bounced off the *Cormorant*'s outer hull, and the whole submarine rocked on its cradle.

On the computer screen was the warning:

"MEDICAL EMERGENCY 571. FOUR MINUTES TO . . ."

For a moment, Captain Cockle stared at the shattered window in surprise. Then suddenly, as the idea flashed across his mind, he started flicking switches on the control panel.

"William!" he shouted into his microphone. "Listen to me!"

Outside, in Sam's pocket, William saw Dennis Pratt grab the shotgun where it had fallen after Mary had dropped it. He saw both Mary and Sam pull themselves to their feet and stare at Pratt as he held the shotgun on them.

"You kids!" he shouted. "Get over here right now!" William felt Sam walking forward.

Suddenly, William heard his grandfather's voice in his radio. For a moment he listened, then he hissed up to Sam, "In a moment, Sam, take me in your hand and run round the edge of the shed – I'll tell you when – do you hear me?"

"But what about Mum and Dad?"

"You'll see. Just trust me. OK?" and he saw the big fat fingers of Sam's right hand reaching up for him.

"That's better," said Dennis Pratt when the whole Sutcliffe family were standing in front of him, in range of the shotgun. "Now, let me tell you something, Mary. I never liked your husband or you and your snotty children. It's just that I could never come up with the ideas for toys that Stephen could, that's all. And even when he did come up with them, he could never see that it would be much easier to sell them straight to the big toy companies than to try and make them ourselves."

"So you did do it, didn't you, Dennis?" said Stephen. "You took my ideas and you sold them without asking me. I suppose you kept all the money as well, didn't you? And then pretended that the company was going broke!"

"That's right!" spat Dennis. "You were never any good at figures, and you would never listen to Mary here when she realised what was going on. You never wanted to make a fuss. Well, now that I have the doll, I don't need to get you to sell the farm so that I can drain the lake and get it back. I'll just take it with me and sell it, and you won't have any proof that it didn't belong to me all along. What do you have to say about that?"

But none of the Sutcliffe family were looking at him any more. They were staring at the shed, at the broken window, and at the strange light coming from inside. Suddenly, with a whirring whoosh and a tinkle of glass, the remains of the window blew out and a strange yellow object shot across the lawn, straight at Dennis Pratt's head.

"Now, Sam! Run!" shouted William.

For a second, Sam Sutcliffe stood rooted to the spot and then, as if he were waking from a dream, he looked at William in his hand and rushed around the shed to the opposite side. On the lawn, Dennis Pratt had ducked to avoid the strange yellow object, giving Stephen and his family time to run for cover. He saw the thing – a new helicopter toy it must have been – dash across the lawn, turn and dive behind the shed, disappear for a moment, and then fly away across the lawn, heading for the power cables.

He gripped the shotgun tighter in his hand, picked up the brief-case from the grass, and started to run. Very well, then, he would grab this new toy and sell it, along with the doll. And the Sutcliffes could take a running jump. He didn't need them any more.

Captain Cockle held the *Cormorant* hovering above Sam's upstretched hand as steady as he could, so that William could climb aboard through the diving hatch.

"Quick!" he shouted over the radio. "We only have three minutes left and hardly enough power!"

"Good luck, Sam!" shouted William back though the open hatch and saw Sam staring up at them as the *Cormorant* tilted forward and zoomed round the shed, heading for the power cables with the two bare copper wires hanging down below.

"Well done, Horatio!" cheered Dr Cockle, looking back out of the porthole.

"We couldn't just sit there and let the Sutcliffes get blasted to bits, now, could we?" said Captain Cockle.

"Not after he stole the doll!" said William.

"And swindled the father!" added Dr Cockle.

"Or planned to drain the pond!" said Jenny.

"Hold tight, everyone. This is going to be a bumpy ride and we have to keep out of Pratt's way until the police arrive. After that, we only have a few minutes of electricity left, and if we can't reach those power lines by then, we're stuck!"

Suddenly, from behind and below, there was the boom of the shotgun.

"Hold tight!" And with a screaming roar a mass of shotgun pellets zoomed past the *Cormorant* a few feet off the starboard side, spinning the flying submarine in their wake.

"My goodness, that was close!"

"Granddad – look at the power!"

A red light was flashing on the centre of the control console and the computer screen read: "POWER LEVEL CRITICAL! BEGIN EMERGENCY DESCENT PROCEDURE IMMEDIATELY. TOTAL POWER FAILURE IN THIRTY SECONDS!"

"A pity we didn't remain plugged in longer than we did," said Captain Cockle. "Now what'll we do?"

"Look!" shouted Dr Cockle.

Silhouetted by the red rays of the setting sun at the far end of the field was the black skeleton of the power pylon, reaching up far into the sky; and from its head, joining it with its fellows, was a set of heavy, hanging power cables.

"William! Are the wires to the batteries still hanging down out of the diving hatch?"

"Yes, Granddad!"

"Right!"

Captain Cockle pulled across the computer keyboard, held the helicopter joystick between his knees to keep the *Cormorant* in level flight, and typed in:

REDUCTION PROGRAMME
ENLARGEMENT FACTOR 30

The words "INSUFFICIENT POWER" flashed on the computer screen, followed by "WARNING – POWER SYSTEM FAILURE IN FIFTEEN SECONDS!"

"We'll see about that," said Captain Cockle and,

gritting his teeth, he turned the *Cormorant* towards the black skeleton of the power pylon.

Dennis Pratt followed the model helicopter across the field, with the shotgun in one hand and the precious brief-case in the other. Out of the corner of his eye, he saw the blue flashing lights of a police car come round the edge of the farmhouse.

"Blast!" He swore to himself. He would never have time to catch the new model now.

He was near the power pylon now and the model helicopter was way up in the darkening sky, high above the cables way out of reach. He could hear the little motor purring away. It was, pity to leave a beautiful new toy like that, but if he wasn't going to be able to steal it and sell it, then Stephen Sutcliffe wasn't going to make any money out of it either.

He took careful aim and fired. The gun kicked in his hand and he could almost see the lead shot zoom skywards and . . . miss the little helicopter.

Blast! Blast! Blast! He would just have to let it go now. It was only a matter of time before the police came looking for him, and if they found him here with the brief-case then they might believe Stephen Sutcliffe's story over his. He took one last look at the beautiful model.

Then, suddenly, its motor stopped!

"Got you!" laughed Mr Pratt cruelly as the little model started to drift down towards him. He put down the shotgun and the brief-case, and held up his arms to catch it.

"Horatio!" cried Dr Cockle.

"Oh, dear! We've run out of power!"

"What'll we do?" asked Jenny.

"We'll have to drift down like a sycamore leaf," said Captain Cockle, wrestling with the controls. "If I tilt the rotors like this, they'll bite into the air and cushion our fall. Now, if I can only pull us over towards those cables. Hold tight, everyone, and close your eyes! Keep your hands away from anything metallic."

Dennis Pratt watched the little model drift down towards the power lines and his outstretched arms. In the light of the setting sun he could just see two thin wires dangling down from it. He was still watching when they touched the power cable and a blinding explosion of white light burst in the dark sky. Lightning arced down the steel of the power pylons, and the air was full of the spit and crackle of electricity that seemed to tear at his clothes and make his hair stand on end. The last thing he remembered before he fainted was the hot sting of sunburn all over his body and hearing the muffled roar of a real, full-sized helicopter directly overhead, blowing him to his knees with the down draught of its rotors.

15

FULL-SIZED AGAIN!

"Help! I've gone blind!" cried Dr Cockle.

"It's your glasses, Granny!" said Jenny. "They're all frosted up. And so are the portholes!"

William gave a yelp of pain from the seat next to her.

"Ouch! Don't touch your seat-belt buckles. They're colder than an ice lolly straight out of the deep-freeze."

"The power's back on!" laughed Captain Cockle in delight. "And we're still airborne. Let's switch on the demister, clear those portholes and see where we are."

As the portholes cleared, they could all see that the *Cormorant* was hovering over a forest bordering a small lake. To their left was a long row of power pylons stretching to the horizon and, beyond them, across a field, was a farmhouse, a farmyard and a shed. The blue flashing lights of a police car blinked against the white stonework and the huddle of people who were gazing up at them.

One small figure near the shed waved.

They were full-sized again!

"Let's land on the other side of this forest and walk back," suggested Dr Cockle. "I really want to find out what was in that brief-case!"

It took Captain Cockle only a few minutes to land the *Cormorant* in a quiet spot between some trees and a disused barn on the other side of the forest from the Sutcliffe's farmhouse. Then he folded up the rotor blades, switched off the engine and the lights, and all four of them trooped round to visit the Sutcliffes.

When they arrived, the blue lights of the police car were flashing even brighter in the twilight. Stephen Sutcliffe and his wife were busy giving statements to a police sergeant, and another policeman was returning across the field with something in his hand.

"Excuse me," said the sergeant on seeing the Cockles. "But can I ask who you are? You see, there's a police investigation going on here."

"My name is Catherine Cockle," explained Dr Cockle. "And this is my husband Horatio, the famous inventor. My grandson William here thinks he lost his model submarine in the pond at the farm, and we've come to see if anyone's found it."

"Well, I'm so sorry!" said Mary Sutcliffe, stepping forward. "But there's been a funny accident with that thing. It flew out of the shed all on its own, just like a helicopter, and crashed into the power lines at the end of the field. And then . . ." Suddenly, Mary Sutcliffe thought how ridiculous this must all sound to somebody who wasn't there at the time to see it.

"You don't believe me, do you?" she said to Dr Cockle.

"Oh, we believe you all right," said Dr Cockle. "Horatio's inventions are always doing things like that. Never mind. I'm sure he can build William another one."

"I'd love to talk to you about that model," said Stephen Sutcliffe. "How did you ever manage to pack so much detail and working parts into a toy as small as that?"

"Ah . . . er . . . I have a talent for making things small . . . I mean a talent for making small things!" said Captain Cockle.

"I know who you really are," said a voice, and there was Abigail with a mischievous gleam in her eye, looking closely at Dr Cockle's torn and stained jacket. "They're really the little people, aren't you?"

"Please excuse Abigail," explained Mary Sutcliffe. "She lives in a world of her own, sometimes."

"Not at all," said Captain Cockle.

Sam tugged at William's arm and beckoned them over to one side, away from the police and the other grown-ups.

"So it worked for you, then," he said. "You got enough electricity from the power lines to get back to full size!"

"We did indeed. Thanks to you!" said William.

"I found this over by the power lines, sergeant," said the other policeman and held up Dennis Pratt's brief-case. "It must be the brief-case you were talking about. But I'm afraid it's locked."

"We'll soon see about that," said Stephen Sutcliffe. "Sam, go and get me the chisel from the shed, please."

Five minutes later, the brief-case was lying open on the Sutcliffes' kitchen table. Inside was a computer disc, a set of rather soggy but quite readable plans, a spare microchip, and the doll that Stephen Sutcliffe had invented. Mary made tea for everyone while Stephen played a hair-drier over the doll and talked to Captain Cockle about model submarines and the problems of using laser beams to open baked bean tins. Then he took a fresh battery from the kitchen drawer, put it into the doll's back and said, "Now, dolly, what is your name, please?"

With a slightly wobbly voice the doll said, "Hello! My name is Abigail. What is yours?"

"There!" said Stephen Sutcliffe. "That's the doll that was stolen, sergeant, and those are the plans and the computer disc."

"This calls for a celebration!" said Dr Cockle. "I'm hungry, after all this excitement. Why don't we order pizza with lots of mushrooms and salami?"

Abigail laughed and clapped her hands. Her mother looked at Dr Cockle as if she was about to ask something.

"I'm sorry this evidence wasn't available the last time we accused Mr Pratt of theft," said Stephen Sutcliffe to the two police officers. "But here it is now, and I would like you to arrest him."

"We would if we could find him," said the sergeant. "Did anyone see where he went?"

When the blinding light faded, Dennis Pratt couldn't see a thing. Sweat had broken out in rivers all over his body and stung his suddenly sunburnt skin. He sat down on the ground heavily, rubbing his eyes and waiting for the blindness to go away. Slowly his vision returned, and he was staring out at the darkening sky from a the strange bowl-shaped dip in the ground he had suddenly found himself in. All around the grass was scorched and brown, but at the edge of the dip it suddenly grew into strange, alien blades of vegetation, each twelve feet high.

Towering above him into the sky, so that its top was lost in the darkening clouds, was the most massive power pylon he had ever seen. It was taller than a hundred oil rigs piled on top of each other and the legs were thicker than office blocks. At the edge of the strange dip was an enormous double